Other books by Alex Ander:

Special Agent Cruz Crime Dramas:
Vengeance Is Mine (Book #1)
Defense of Innocents (Book #2)
Plea for Justice (Book #3)

Aaron Hardy Patriotic Thrillers:
The Unsanctioned Patriot (Book #1)
American Influence (Book #2)
Deadly Assignment (Book #3)
Patriot Assassin (Book #4)
The Nemesis Protocol (Book #5)
Necessary Means (Book #6)
Foreign Soil (Book #7)

Standalone:
The President's Man: Aaron Hardy Omnibus 1-3
The President's Man 2: Aaron Hardy Omnibus 4-6
Special Agent Cruz Crime Series
The First Agents

Vengeance Is Mine

FBI
Action & Adventure

Alex Ander

Copyright ©2017 Jason A. Burley
All rights reserved. No portion of this publication may be reproduced or transmitted in any form or by any means without permission, except by a reviewer who may quote brief passages in a review to be published in a newspaper, magazine or electronically via the Internet.

This book is a work of fiction. All names, characters, places and incidents are the products of the author's imagination or are used fictitiously. Any similarities to real events or locations or actual persons, living or dead, is entirely coincidental.

Chapter 1: Cabin

January 7th, 5:32 p.m.
18 miles southwest of Tallahassee, Florida
Near the eastern edge of the Apalachicola National Forest

Special Agent Raychel Elisa DelaCruz opened the trunk of her black Dodge Charger, slipped her arms out of her dark blue blazer and tossed the garment into the compartment. She grabbed a bulletproof vest, the letters **FBI** emblazoned on the front, and handed it to her partner. She donned a similar vest over her pastel blue blouse, cinched the straps and pulled her ponytail from under the protective apparel. She inserted a communication device into her ear, tapped the earpiece and glanced toward her partner. "Check, check...one—two—three."

Special Agent Curtis Ashford paused from securing the straps on his vest only long enough to give her the 'thumbs-up' sign. "I'm reading you loud and clear, Cruz."

During her time in the military, her fellow soldiers called her Cruz. They had joked that her full name was too difficult to pronounce. To this day, the nickname had stuck and everyone who knew her used the shortened version of her name.

Ashford double-checked the status of his Glock 22 and shoved it into his hip holster before touching the spare magazines on his left hip. He stared over the trunk lid toward the winding dirt road that led to a small shabby cabin, surrounded by dense woods. "We really should call this in and wait for backup."

Cruz's reply was sharp and monotone. "We probably should." She dropped the magazine from her Glock 23 pistol into her hand. Verifying the magazine's capacity, she rammed it into the butt of her weapon and pulled back on the weapon's slide. Seeing a shiny brass case in the chamber, she let go of the slide, holstered the Glock and adjusted the black belt supporting the hardware and her dark blue slacks.

Ashford curled up the right side of his mouth. "Something tells me we're not going to do that though, are we?" Not getting a reply, he studied the woods on either side of the long driveway. Darkness enveloped the vegetation a few feet inside the tree line. "If anyone slips past us," he lifted his chin toward the forest, "it's going to be hard to find them in this."

Cruz tapped the button on the back of her Surefire flashlight and a brief beam of white light appeared inside the trunk. She closed the lid, stowed the flashlight and observed the surrounding area. "Then, I guess we'll have to make sure no one slips past us." Ashford's tone and body language compelled her to offer assurances. "We've done this before, Ash...rolled up on scenes and taken down the bad guys *without* calling in the cavalry." She motioned toward the direction of the cabin. "Peterson and Lopez are up there and I'm not going to let them get away again." She gave him the 'peace' sign. "Two times is two times too many. One way or another, this ends...*tonight*."

"I'm with you on that, Cruz. My concern is...what if there are more people than just Peterson and Lopez up there?"

"Our recon says otherwise." Hidden among the trees, Cruz and Ashford had watched the cabin for an hour and had only seen two men inside the structure.

Standing at the right-rear corner of the Charger, she squinted at her partner. His black hair, dark eyes and long eyelashes gave him a hardened, attractive appearance. The square jaw and perpetual stubble on his cheeks only added to his 'bad boy' good looks. He was not her type, but she was confident he had no trouble getting dates.

Wearing navy blue slacks, a white shirt under his bulletproof vest and black shoes, Curtis Ashford stood six-feet tall and weighed two hundred pounds. He had an athletic frame with wide shoulders, a narrow waist and heavily muscled arms and legs. A football player in college, he made the team as a linebacker. To him, the best part of the game was hitting people. His coaches had determined he was too small to play linebacker and moved him to running back. Disappointed at first, he soon discovered he could fulfill his hitting prerequisite at the new position. He ran over and through defenders on his way to a school rushing record in his first year. A knee injury in the playoffs ended his college career, in addition to his hopes of playing professional football. With his dreams sidelined, he focused on a backup plan—becoming an FBI agent.

"You know I'm always ready for a good fight, Cruz."

Aware of his penchant for getting physical with criminals and uncooperative suspects, Cruz grinned. *That's an understatement.*

"I just want to know what your plan is if this thing goes south." He saw Cruz's grin transition into a smile. He rolled his eyes. "So, it's going to be like all the other times. We pull plan 'B' out of our butts." Shaking his head, he drew his pistol. "Okay, let's do this." Ashford extended his arm. "Ladies first...lead the way."

... ...

The single-level cabin was made of old wooden planks, dried and cracked from countless years of being unprotected from the elements. Many of the boards were split at the ends. Long gaps appeared where the edges of the wood were joined. Hastily constructed patch jobs could be seen on all sides of the building, ranging from irregular-shaped pieces of plywood nailed to the sides to rags and cardboard stuck into the smaller gaps. The techniques did little to keep out the weather, and the abundant critters looking for food or shelter.

A short porch, less than a foot off the ground, jutted out four feet from the front door and spread out eight feet to the left and right. The handrails that enclosed the porch were made of a rotted horizontal two-by-four resting on several shorter vertical two-by-fours. None of the timber had been painted or stained.

Each side of the cabin had a window at shoulder-height, while the back of the building had a door and a three-step staircase leading to the ground, which sloped away from the back door. White smoke billowed out of the brick chimney on the left side of the cabin. The column drifted to the left every few seconds from an intermittent, faint breeze.

A green Ford truck with larger than normal tires and a lift kit was backed against the porch on the right side of the door. The tree line on the sides and back of the cabin was no more than twenty feet from the shack. The distance from the tree line, near the driveway, to the porch was closer to a hundred feet and the terrain afforded no natural cover. Cruz and Ashford knelt within the cover of the trees to the left of the driveway, studying the cabin and the immediate area. She had half thought about using her Charger to make the approach, but the roar of the engine would have made it more challenging to maintain the element of surprise.

Ashford spoke, his voice hushed. "It'll be dark soon. Are we going in under the cover of night?"

Cruz shook her head. "I want a little bit of daylight left, in case this thing doesn't go according to plan."

"Speaking of this plan...care to share?"

She made an arc with her left arm. "You go left and take the back door. Stay in the trees as long as you can before you make your approach." Nodding toward the cabin, she added, "I'll be knocking on the front door."

"What's our R-O-E?"

"Rules of Engagement haven't changed. We fire if they fire at us. I want them to stand trial for what they've done."

United States Border Patrol agents Stephen Peterson and Marcus Lopez had been using their positions of authority to help smuggle drugs and illegal immigrants across the Mexican-American border. Their activities had been on the FBI's radar for several months, while the agency gathered evidence against the pair. They fled a day ahead of a scheduled raid to apprehend them, moving deeper into the country, finally settling at this location.

"That being said—" Cruz plopped her hand onto Ashford's shoulder to get his attention. "You're cleared to go hot." She poked him in the chest. "Be careful. These people are well-trained agents and they know how to shoot. We're both going home tonight. *Got it?*" When she did not get a reply, Cruz re-stated her question. "Are we clear, Ash?"

He smiled. Cruz was four years his elder and he sometimes felt as if she treated him like a younger brother, protecting him from schoolyard bullies or reminding him to look both ways before crossing the street. If any other person had treated him that way, he or she would have been on the receiving end of a severe tongue-lashing. Cruz was exempt, however. Secretly, he enjoyed her concern for his well-being. While growing up, Ashford, the youngest of four male siblings, never had anyone to shield him from the incessant teasing from his older brothers.

He nodded and gave *his interpretation* of her instructions. "We shoot first, ask questions later, and go home with no new holes in our bodies...Got it." He leapt to his feet. "I'll let you know when I'm in position. Watch yourself, Cruz."

Cruz shook her head and grinned, while her partner disappeared into the thick foliage. His imposing presence and sense of humor had cultivated in her mind the persona of a big teddy bear. He portrayed the image of a tough and surly man, while maintaining his fun-loving and joking demeanor.

Minutes later, her earpiece crackled.

"I'm in position and ready to breach on your order."

"Copy that. Stand by. I'm moving out." Cruz took one more look around the area and slipped out of the concealment of the underbrush. Crouching, she sprinted toward the cabin. Fifteen feet away from the truck, Ashford's voice came over the airwaves.

"I've got movement in the house...Someone's heading for the front door."

Cruz darted to her right and dropped to the ground, using the truck as a barricade. As long as no one stepped too far out onto the porch, she would not be seen. The door to the cabin opened and closed. Boots scuffed along the wooden boards, creaking under a heavy weight. Thirty seconds passed. Her pulse was pounding in her head. She had no clear view of the man, but she could see smoke rising from beyond the hood of the truck. *He's having a cigarette. Okay, just finish your smoke and go back inside...No need to step off the porch...No need to...*The door opened and closed again. Cruz waited.

"All clear, Cruz. Two subjects in the structure. You're good to go...over."

Cruz got to her hands and knees and slowly lifted her body to see over the hood of the truck. *He's gone.* She raced toward the truck, stopping in front of the vehicle's grill. Easing to her left, she peeked around the right corner. No one was in sight. She moved back in front of the grill and withdrew a folding knife from her pocket. She thumbed the blade and it automatically locked open. "I'll be ready to go in two minutes."

"Copy that."

... ...

Stephen Peterson closed the door to the cabin and trotted across the main room. "Get your crap together. We're bugging out." He grabbed a duffle bag, dropped it onto the table and started tossing in stacks of hundred-dollar bills. He paused to point at the cache of weapons and ammunition in the corner of the room. "Grab as much ammo as you can."

"What the hell are you talking about?" Lopez had joined him at the table.

Peterson jerked his thumb over his shoulder. "There's somebody out there. I can feel it and I can *smell* it." His ten years of service, guarding the border between the United States and Mexico had ingrained in him a sense of when others were nearby. Spending many nights on patrols, he knew when people were lurking in the dark, waiting for him to move to another position, so they could sneak into the country. Eventually, he gave up and decided to make money from the activities. His choice had gotten him and his friend in their current situation.

"So, now you can *smell* when people are around." Lopez stared at Peterson. "I think you've been on the run so long, looking over your shoulder, you're seeing ghosts."

Peterson stopped stuffing the money stacks and held Lopez's gaze. "I went for a smoke and I could smell perfume. When was the last time the forest smelled like perfume?"

Lopez laughed. "You've got to be kidding me. You're spooked because you think you smelled *perfume*. That's what this is all about?" He shook his head. "No, it couldn't be flowers or—"

"Shut up and get the damn ammo." Peterson zipped the duffle bag and slung it over his shoulder before checking the status of his pistol. He jumped and nearly sent a round into the floor when he heard a fist pounding on the front door, followed by a commanding female voice.

∞ ∞ ∞ ∞ ∞ ∞ ∞

Chapter 2: Surrounded

Special Agent Cruz issued a command, her voice as deep as she could make it. "This is the FBI. The place is surrounded. There's nowhere to go. Come out with your hands up."

Peterson shot a glance at Lopez and raised his pistol toward the door. He aimed left of the door, then right of it. *She'll be on one side or the other, but not in front of it.* He swung the pistol back to the left. "Aw, to hell with it," he said and repeatedly pulled the trigger, while strafing the front of the cabin. The slide locked back. He inserted a fresh magazine and charged toward the door, firing as he ran.

... ...

Squatting near the stairs at the back of the structure, Ashford heard Cruz pummel the front door. Her voice travelled electronically to one ear; live to the other. "This is the FBI. The place is surrounded. There's nowhere to go. Come out with your hands up." He cocked his head. *'The place is surrounded?' It's just the two of us.*

He sprang forward and reached the back door in three giant steps. Pressing his back to the wall, he heard gunfire. Wheeling around, he put a size-twelve-foot to the door and the rickety barrier flew inward. The top hinge separated from the doorjamb and the door listed to the right. He raised his weapon and had both Peterson and Lopez in his sights. They were running toward the front door. He charged forward and yelled, "Freeze...FBI...don't move."

Ashford watched Lopez spin to his right with pistol in hand. He did not give the man a second chance to comply with his order, pressing the trigger when Lopez's chest was centered in his sights.

Lopez continued his turn. Instead of penetrating his chest, the bullet zipped across it, leaving a half-inch wide trench from his sternum to his right nipple before lodging in his bicep. Screaming, he dropped to the floor and dragged himself toward the out-of-reach pistol. Flopping forward the wounded arm, his fingertips touched the butt of the weapon. Before he could grasp it, searing pain radiated from the hand and through the arm. His head reeled backward.

Ashford had stomped on Lopez's hand with the heel of his dress shoe before shifting most of his bodyweight forward. "Marcus Lopez, you're under arrest for the illegal smuggling of drugs, weapons and immigrants. You have the right to remain silent..."

Lopez howled, while tears moistened his reddening cheeks.

Shrugging his shoulders, Ashford handcuffed Lopez and said, "...Or not," before informing the man of the rest of his rights.

... ...

Cruz stood to the left of the door, balled her fist and rapped on the wooden door. "This is the FBI. The place is surrounded. There's nowhere to go. Come out with your hands up." She took a two-handed grip on her Glock and waited, her back pressed against the cabin, her left ear facing the dwelling. She opened her mouth, but before she could issue another command bullets flew out of the cabin, starting on the other side of the door, heading straight for her. She whipped her head around and dove to the right. Landing on her right side, she shielded her head and face from the debris. Splinters from the handrails flew into the air, as bullets zipped through the old wood. Having taken three rounds in her back, her chest heaved and her mind went back to an encounter during her days as an officer for her hometown police department of Dalhart, Texas.

Two years into her job with the Dalhart Police Department, she made a routine traffic stop of a vehicle with a broken taillight. The incident marked the first time she had drawn her weapon and exchanged gunfire with a criminal, who happened to be a Mexican drug trafficker on the FBI's Most Wanted List. A bullet had grazed the surface of her leg, but she was able to capture and arrest the fugitive, shooting and wounding two of his companions. Cruz received special recognition from the FBI and the Dalhart P.D. promoted her to sergeant. Until this moment, that was the only time she had been shot.

Cruz drew a deep breath, but the pain in her chest forced her to abort the process. She settled for shorter gulps of air. The bullets had ceased flying, so she rolled onto her back and extended her firearm toward the door. She let out a yelp when her back touched the porch. *Bad idea, Raychel.* Continuing the roll, she propped herself on her left elbow. A second wave of gunfire commenced. More holes appeared on the door. Dust, dirt and fragments flew outward.

Digging the right heel of her black chunky one-inch high heels into the brittle planks, she scooted backwards, until she came to the end of the porch, her upper body thrust against the bowing handrail. A split-second later, the door exploded when Peterson's bulk crashed through it. Cruz saw the slide locked back on his weapon and slid her index finger from the trigger to the frame. She shouted. Still recovering from being shot, her commands were mixed with coughs. "Stop...right...there."

Peterson let go of his sidearm, leapt from the porch and landed in the bed of the truck. Scrambling over the side, he climbed into the driver's seat and cranked the engine.

Cruz struggled to get to a standing position. With every movement, the sharp needle-like sensations pricked her back. Taking inventory of her injuries, she felt lucky. Ashford appeared on the porch and dashed to her side. His voice was strained when he addressed her.

"Cruz, are you hurt? Are you okay? Did he shoot you?" Bobbing his head up and down and flicking his eyes left and right, he searched for bullet wounds.

Bent over and her head hanging down, she waved him off. "I'm good. I took them in the vest." She coughed. "I'm good." Her left arm jerked toward the truck. "Take the left side. I'll come up on the right." Ashford ran toward the handrail on the opposite side of the porch, crashing through it, instead of going over it. Cruz rose to her full height, arched her back and leaned from side to side. Having cut the fuel line on the truck, she was in no hurry to go after Peterson. He was going nowhere and his empty weapon was lying on the porch. With a two-handed grip on her service weapon, she took the single step off the porch and drew alongside the right window of the truck, staying several feet back from the door.

Since getting into the truck, Peterson had been cranking the engine nonstop. Groaning, the battery hardly had enough power to engage the starter. He turned the key again, but all he heard were the commands of Special Agent Cruz.

"End of the line, Peterson." Cruz was staring at him over the sights of her pistol. She shifted her eyes to the left. Ashford had drawn up on the left side of the truck, stopping short of creating a deadly crossfire situation between the two of them. "Exit the vehicle with your hands up."

Peterson rotated his head to the left and stared down the muzzle of Ashford's pistol. He swung his head back toward Cruz. His mind searched for any weapons he may have stashed on his person or in the truck—*nothing*. He was not stupid. He had no cards to play and he knew it.

"Hands, Peterson...I need to see those hands." Fixing her gaze on Peterson, Cruz's eyes narrowed.

"And, if I see *anything* in them...it won't end well for you."

Ashford barked a similar command, but his voice boomed in the stillness of the quiet night. "Get out, now!"

Peterson raised his right hand, while opening the door with his left. He swung his legs outward and slid out of the seat, while Ashford took a step backward.

Cruz moved around the front of the truck, stopping at the left corner. "On your knees...get on your knees."

Peterson was out of options, but he was not going to go out without some satisfaction. His hands at his sides, barely above his waist, he pivoted to face his female opponent. A crooked grin formed on his lips. "*You* get on your knees, bit—"

Ashford had advanced and driven his foot into the back of Peterson's knee, dropping him and cutting him off in mid-sentence. Ashford followed with a blow to the back of Peterson's head, propelling the disgraced border guard forward, until he was sprawled on the ground, face-first in a spread-eagle position. "That's no way to talk to a lady, Stevie."

Cruz lifted her head and stared at her partner. Ashford saw her. "What?"

"You just *have* to hit someone, don't you?" Shaking her head, she holstered her gun, retrieved her handcuffs and circled around Peterson.

"Hey, he shot you," growled Ashford. "He's lucky to be still sucking wind."

Cruz planted her left knee into her quarry's lower back and clamped a handcuff onto his right wrist. "Stephen Peterson, you have the right to remain silent." She brought his hands behind his back and smacked the second handcuff around his left wrist. "Anything you say can and will be used against you…"

∞ ∞ ∞ ∞ ∞ ∞ ∞

Chapter 3: Refreshed

January 9th, 8:39 a.m.
Washington, D.C.

Special Agent Cruz yawned, blinked and stretched her arms and legs, dragging them across the smooth bed sheets. Shoving her arm under the covers, she ran her fingers up and down her leg, feeling the prickly hairs. Certain tasks were neglected when chasing criminals across the country for several days at a time.

After arresting the border patrol agents, Cruz and Ashford handed off the mundane administrative tasks to the first FBI team to arrive at the cabin. Deciding to stay in Florida and drive back to Washington, D.C. in the morning, they booked two hotel rooms. The next day, they took turns driving and made the fifteen-hour trek in fourteen-and-a-half hours. Closing the front door to her house around Midnight, Cruz had headed for the only place she wanted to be—her bedroom, specifically, her bed. Taking only enough time to strip out of her clothes, use the facilities and slip into a red satin teddy, she was asleep minutes after her body slid beneath the covers.

Cruz grabbed her cell phone from the nightstand, hoping to see she had missed a call from her boyfriend. She had called Derek several times on the long drive home. Each attempt went to voicemail. They had last spoken three days ago. He said he was going out of town for a business meeting. At least that is what she *thought* he had said. She had been searching a hideout used by Peterson and Lopez. Distracted, her focus was not on the phone call. Since Derek worked in international banking, the out-of-town meeting was plausible.

Derek and Cruz had been dating for more than two months and she felt ready to take their relationship to the next level. For her, that meant taking him to meet her mother. She had dated many men, but none came close to making it this far with her. Cruz had never introduced any of her boyfriends to her mother. That was a sacred moment, not to be squandered on the wrong man. Derek might be the one with whom she would spend the rest of her life. She was getting ahead of herself, but falling in love did that to people.

Yawning, Cruz scanned her text messages. "They can wait," she murmured, her voice gravelly. Before she could put the phone on the nightstand, it vibrated and she flinched. Scratching her head, she cleared her throat. "What's up, Ash?"

"Good morning, Cruz."

She caught the distraction in his voice.

"I wanted to give you a heads-up...the director wants to...meet with us this morning...ten o'clock in his office."

Cruz took the phone away from her ear and checked the time. "Where are you?"

"I'm at the office."

"You're at work already? Did you even go home last night and get some sleep?"

"Of course," he said, giving Cruz his full attention. "I'm not as old as you. I understand you folks need more sleep."

Cruz let a puff of air slip past her lips and chuckled. She heard Ashford's smile and let him revel in his verbal victory.

"Besides, I thought I'd get started on the paperwork."

Bless you. Cruz hated paperwork. She never ceased to be amazed at how the simplest of tasks required multiple forms being filled-out and submitted. No one ever warned her about that aspect of law enforcement. "Do you have any idea why he wants to see us?"

"Not a clue," replied Ashford, his distraction returning. "I need to put the finishing touches...on this masterpiece...I'll see you at ten."

"Thanks, Ash." She disconnected the call and tossed the phone onto her bed before shuffling into the bathroom, located off the bedroom. Standing at the sink, she looked at her reflection in the mirror.

Two months ago, Cruz celebrated her twenty-ninth birthday. Despite the last couple of rough days, she felt great. Her slim, well-toned five-foot, eight-inch figure proved she had taken care of her body throughout the years. Falling well below her shoulders, her dark brown hair matched her equally beautiful set of dark brown eyes. She had a long face with high cheekbones and a flawless complexion.

She turned her head from side to side, while turning on the faucet. Bending over to splash water on her face, her back muscles seized and she clutched the sides of the sink. She arched her back and tilted her head backward. Her face contorted and the memories of taking down Peterson and Lopez flooded her mind, especially the three shots to the bulletproof vest. Letting go of the sink with one hand, she pulled the teddy off, drew back her long hair and eyed the damage in the mirror. Three red welts, forming a triangle, were centered above the small of her back. The act of twisting her torso to see over her shoulder sent new shockwaves of discomfort to her brain. She expanded her lungs and exhaled, the air whistling through pursed lips. She let the teddy drop to the floor, grabbed a razor and eased her body into the shower.

Twenty minutes later, Cruz felt refreshed. The hotter than usual water had loosened the muscles in her back and relieved the pain. Wearing a basic white bra and cotton high-cut briefs, she slid hangers left and right along the metal bar inside the bedroom closet. Selecting a matching red blazer and slacks, she laid the outfit on the bed. *After three days of wearing dark colors, I need to brighten things up a bit.* She added a black form-fitting turtleneck sweater and black chunky one-inch high heels to the ensemble before getting dressed, securing her hair in a mid-rise ponytail and heading downstairs to the kitchen. After a breakfast of scrambled eggs and toast, she left the house.

∞ ∞ ∞ ∞ ∞ ∞ ∞

Chapter 4: Take the Day

9:58 a.m.
J. Edgar Hoover Building
Washington, D.C.

Phillip Jameson sat at his desk. He split his attention between examining the contents of a case file and writing on a notepad. He pushed aside a piece of paper and picked up an eight-by-ten photo. His eyes narrowed and he pursed his lips. The photo depicted an attractive woman wearing a two-piece bathing suit. In red marker, a childlike drawing of a crown had been added above the woman's head. To the right of the crown, also in red marker, the word 'winner' was printed. Jameson placed the print to the left and continued thumbing through the rest of the pages.

FBI Director Phillip Jameson had recently turned fifty, though no one could have guessed his age. He was physically fit, following an exercise regimen of weightlifting and jogging. He stood five-feet, eleven-inches tall and weighed one hundred and ninety pounds. He was bald and wore rounded, rectangular eyeglasses with thick black frames. His work attire consisted of a black suit, black shoes, white shirt and a red tie. He changed the shade and print of the tie, but the color was always red. His clothing was a projection of what could be expected from him—a man who displayed impeccable leadership and decision-making skills, while demanding his agents uphold the same high standard of integrity.

For the next couple of minutes, he added to his notes. Hearing a knock on his office door, he paused, glanced at the digital clock on his desk and went back to writing. "The door's open."

Special Agents Cruz and Ashford entered. Ashford closed the door, while Cruz slipped between two straight-back chairs, facing Jameson's desk. She smiled. "Good morning, sir. You wanted to see us."

Not looking up, Jameson pointed with his pen. "Have a seat."

Cruz sat in the chair to Jameson's left and crossed her legs, resting her hands on her thigh. She saw Ashford claim the other chair.

Jameson let go of the pen, put his eyeglasses on the notepad and rocked backward in his chair. Letting out a sigh, he rubbed his eyes with the heels of his hands. Righting himself, he donned his eyeglasses and skimmed the contents of the file folder. "I got a call from a friend of mine—" Jameson stopped short. "First of all, I want to congratulate the both of you on apprehending Peterson and Lopez."

"Thank you, sir."

"Yes, thank you, sir," replied Ashford, crossing his legs.

"It's good to know they're out of play." Jameson took a hard look at his agents. "I know you've got to be tired after all the hours you've spent tracking them down."

Remembering their phone call and Ashford's age-related joke, Cruz shot a sideways glance at him.

Jameson picked up the photo from the file folder. "However, I need you two to do me a favor. As I started to say, a friend of mine, the sheriff of a small town to the north, contacted me about a body discovered this morning. I'd like you to head up there and see if you can help him out with the investigation."

"Do we have jurisdictional authority?"

Jameson shook his head.

"Is the victim somehow connected to the government?"

Jameson held up his hands. "That hasn't been determined yet."

Cruz glanced toward Ashford. "Sir, with all due respect, how does a small-town murder case involve the FBI? We have enough work to keep us busy. Let the locals take care of their own problems." She was familiar with what happened when federal agents showed up at local investigations. The hometown police were never pleased and usually became obstacles in the pursuit of justice. Still tired, she was not feeling up to going toe-to-toe with a sheriff and his deputies.

Jameson rotated the photograph and set it on the opposite edge of his desk, facing her. "This was found on the body."

Cruz uncrossed her legs and leaned forward to see the image. Her body stiffened. "*That* was found with the victim?"

Jameson nodded. "I thought you'd be interested."

Cruz squinted. "It could be a coincidence. It might not mean anything."

"Or, it *could* mean something."

Ashford pinched the picture between his thumb and forefinger and leaned backward. "Whoa, she's *hot*. Is she a witness?"

Jameson ordered the pieces of paper and slid them into the file folder.

Ashford let out a low whistle. "I'm not sure I've seen a skimpier bathing suit." He whipped his head toward Cruz. "I call dibs on the interview."

Cruz's cheeks flushed and she felt her body perspiring. "*Give me that.*" She snatched the photo from his hands. "Show some professionalism." She placed it on the desk, face down.

Ashford shied away, his head cocked, eyebrows arched.

Trying to re-collect her composure, Cruz resumed a relaxed posture and crossed her legs. "Is there anything else, sir?"

"It's all in here." Jameson handed over the file folder. "You can review it on your way up there. Take the day and meet with the sheriff. Maybe you can shed some light on what happened."

Taking the cue the meeting was over, Cruz and Ashford stood. She hung back, while Ashford made his way to the door. Retrieving an envelope from the pocket of her suit coat, she placed it on the Director's nameplate and walked away.

"What's this?" Jameson flipped over the envelope and saw his name written on it.

Reaching the doorway, Cruz spun around and lifted her chin toward him. "Open it and find out, sir."

He pushed aside the unsealed flap and slid out a simple light blue greeting card. In dark black ink, the numbers five and zero took up most of the cover. He opened the card and read it to himself: *...is the new 39!* At the bottom was handwritten: *Happy Birthday, Cruz*

Cruz saw a barely perceptible grin flash across his face.

He regarded his agent. "How'd you find out?" Jameson had never celebrated a birthday at work. He had kept the date, today's date, to himself. He was a private person and did not like people making a fuss over him.

She shrugged. "You're not the only one who has contacts in the bureau." Beaming, she left the office.

He read the card again. This time, alone in his office, he allowed himself to show a real smile. His joy did not come from the wit of the card maker. He could not care less about his age. It was only a number. No, he was happy Cruz had taken the time to remember him, even managing to do so without drawing unwanted attention. He carefully situated the card in front of the clock on his desk, so he would see it whenever he checked the time.

∞ ∞ ∞ ∞ ∞ ∞ ∞

Chapter 5: Burden

11:11 a.m.
Interstate 270 North
45 minutes outside of Washington, D.C.

After hearing the first few words of Derek's outgoing voicemail message, Special Agent Cruz pressed a button on the dashboard of her Charger, ending the call. Her irritation with him for not taking her calls had morphed into worry. Something must be wrong. The twisted knots in her stomach had been telling her the same thing. He had taken several business trips during their relationship and he always managed to contact her.

Okay, Raychel, calm down and take a breath. It's only been three days. He could be...tied up in meetings and unable to break away. He could be... She exhaled slowly. *Relax. He's fine. Don't jump to conclusions.* Curling her fingers around the turn signal lever, she checked her side mirror, changed lanes and passed a slow-moving vehicle.

"I can't put my finger on it, but there's something about this picture that's familiar."

Cruz shot a glance to her right. Since leaving Washington, D.C. forty-five minutes ago, Ashford had been reviewing the file from Jameson. Most of that time had been spent staring at the photograph of the woman.

"This seems to have been taken years ago, but I feel like I know her." Cupping his chin, he paused. "Usually, I never forget a face." He turned toward Cruz and lifted his eyebrows twice before adding, "Or, in her case, a *body.*"

Feeling her body temperature rising, Cruz twisted the fan knob to the left and moved the heat selector closer to the blue section. She squirmed in her seat and arched her back, trying to relieve pressure points. Out of the corner of her eye, she saw Ashford had the picture inches away from his face, squinting. The only thing missing was a Sherlock Holmes hat and magnifying glass. She touched her cheek with the back of her cold hand. The coolness felt good. The reflection in the rear view mirror showed her crimson face.

"It's like when you're trying to remember a song or an actor's name. It's right there on the tip—"

Cruz cut him off, making no effort to mask her annoyance. "I'm sure there's other information in that folder you could be reading, instead of drooling over that picture. Honestly, you're acting like some horny teenager, who got a hold of a Victoria's Secret catalog."

Ashford rotated his upper body toward his partner and leaned against the door. His mouth agape and his eyes reduced to slits, he stared at her. *What the hell is your problem?* He re-phrased the question when he uttered it aloud. "What's your problem, Cruz?" He held up his index finger. "First, you bark at me in Jameson's office and now you rip me a new one over," he lifted the photo in his hand, "looking at a hot girl." He shook his head. "What did I do? If you got something to say to me, spit it out. We've known each other long enough that I think we can be straight and say what's on our minds." He held his hands up. "What's got you so pi—"

"It's not you," interrupted Cruz, her voice dropping an octave. "It's me."

Ashford's shoulders relaxed. More questions formed in his mind. "All right, what did *you* do that's got you so upset?"

Cruz shook her head, took the print from him and held it up to his face. "No, I meant it's *me*." She waved the image back and forth. "*This*...is *me*. I'm the one you've been staring at for the last hour." She dropped the photograph into his lap and grasped the steering wheel with both hands, her knuckles turning white.

Ashford flipped over the print. Studying it, his next words leapt from his mouth. "You're Miss Texas?" The woman in the picture had a sash across her body with the words 'Miss Texas' on the sash.

Staring straight ahead, Cruz nodded.

He held the photo between them. His eyes moving left and right, he saw the resemblance.

She filled in the blanks for him. "That was taken eleven years ago at the Miss America Pageant. It was a publicity shot. I was eighteen at the time."

"Whoa, wait a minute." Ashford made a 'T' with his hands. "I have to call timeout here." He pointed at her. "You're telling me *you* were Miss Texas." He jabbed his finger at the image of Cruz, specifically, the word 'winner.' "And, you went on to win the Miss America Pageant at the age of eighteen. Wow. I can't believe I'm sitting next to a beauty queen. This is unbelievable. Why didn't you ever tell me? We're partners. That's something I should know, don't you think?"

"I didn't *win*. I placed *second* at the pageant. And, I didn't tell you about it for the same reason I don't tell anyone about it. When people find out, they have the same reaction you just had." Cruz rolled her head. "*Wow*, she's a *beauty queen*. Their minds shut off and that's all they can see. I've lived with the narrow-mindedness for ten years. I'm sick of it. So, you'll have to forgive me if I don't necessarily want to talk about those days of my life." Silence consumed the interior of the Charger for nearly a minute.

"I'm sorry, Cruz," Ashford said, backpedalling. "I had no idea."

Hearing the sullen tone in his voice, she felt terrible for yelling at him. It was not his fault. He had no way of knowing she was the woman in the picture, or about the life challenges associated with having participated in talent contests.

"I can't imagine what you've had to endure." He held up his right index finger. "You've served your country in the military." The middle finger was extended. "You made sergeant for the Dalhart Police Department." The ring finger was added. "You apprehended a Mexican drug trafficker, got the attention of the FBI and went on to become a top notch FBI agent."

Cruz tilted her head and frowned. *What kind of apology is this?*

Ashford rattled off several additional accolades, including her bringing to justice a member of congress involved in a sex scandal. All digits on his right hand were extended. The last three fingers on his left hand pointed upward, while he pinched the photo with the first two. "I'm running out of fingers here, Cruz."

She faced him, but kept her eyes on the road. "You're not very good at apologies. You know that, right?"

He ignored the question. "Add to your list of accomplishments a Miss Texas title and runner-up in the biggest talent contest in the country and..." he sighed and motioned toward her. "Your shoulders must be sore from carrying around the burden of all that success. I really am sorry. I can see you've had a *tough* life."

She glanced at him to verify the sarcasm in his voice.

"I guess all that's missing in your life is fortune." He held her gaze. "That is, unless you're going to tell me you had a wealthy uncle and he left you a boatload of money."

Cruz raised her eyebrows. "Are you finished?"

"No, not yet," he countered. "You've accomplished more in ten years than most people do in a lifetime. You're smart, kindhearted and a damn good FBI agent. If people can't see those qualities in you," he shrugged and raised his voice, "*to hell with them.* They're not worth your time. Your past is your past. It's a part of who you are. Embrace it and be proud of what you've done."

Cruz navigated the Charger into the far right lane, preparing to take the exit for Interstate 70, the Dwight D. Eisenhower Highway, south of Frederick, Maryland. Once they were past the hectic traffic of the interchange, she rolled her head toward Ashford. "Thank you. That means a lot to me. It really does." She watched him flash a smile and nod.

A few miles down the highway, Ashford picked up the photo. "I just realized why I didn't recognize you."

Hearing his tone, Cruz braced for an off-color joke.

He stroked his chin before wagging his finger at the image. "You're not wearing your Glock."

Her jaw muscles relaxed and she checked the side mirror.

Ashford grinned and added, "*Although*...there's not a whole lot of fabric there to hold up a gun."

She whipped her head toward him, the redness returning to her cheeks. Lines formed on her forehead.

Noticing the feigned anger, Ashford could not resist dumping fuel onto the fire. "I suppose you could've slipped the muzzle," he motioned with his right hand, "under the side ties of your G-string bikini."

"That's it." Cruz yanked the photo from his hand and held it up. "No more looking at this. In fact, you're to forget you ever saw it. Are we clear?" She tucked the image under her leg.

Ashford's chest rocked up and down. After several moments, he brought his hilarity to a snicker. "Sorry, Cruz, it's too late. That image's been burned into my brain." Chuckling, he added, "When my head hits the pillow and I close my eyes, tonight..." His voice trailed off and he pointed toward her thigh, the one concealing the photo. When she cocked her head toward him and rolled her eyes, his amusement returned in full force.

Cruz looked at the clock on the dashboard—11:27. They would be arriving at their destination, Huntingdon, Pennsylvania, in about two hours.

∞ ∞ ∞ ∞ ∞ ∞ ∞

Chapter 6: Huntingdon

1:31 p.m.
Sheriff's Office
Huntingdon, Pennsylvania

Sheriff Corbin Decker took a big bite of his grilled ham and cheese sandwich before returning his attention to the case file in front of him. Two bites later, he washed down the food with a couple gulps from a twenty-ounce bottle of pop. Reaching for the sandwich, he heard a knock on the office door. He peered through the window and motioned for the man, standing on the other side of the glass, to enter. "Come in." Decker took another bite of his sandwich and grabbed a napkin.

Special Agent Cruz stepped into the sheriff's office, followed by Curtis Ashford, who closed the door behind him. She presented her FBI credentials. "Sheriff Decker," she motioned toward Ashford, "this is Special Agent Curtis Ashford and I'm—"

"Special Agent Raychel DelaCruz," said Decker, nodding his head and wiping his mouth with the napkin. "I was wondering if I would be getting a visit from you." After shaking her hand, he gestured toward the chair facing his desk. "Please have a seat." Pointing toward the corner near the door, he added, "There's another chair for you Agent..."

"Ashford...Curtis Ashford," said Cruz's partner, shaking the sheriff's hand.

"Of course, please draw up a chair." Decker sat and moved his food aside. "You'll have to excuse me. Some days I have to squeeze in a bite whenever I get the time."

Cruz smiled. "I know what you mean. I'm sure with all that's happened around here, it's been a hectic day."

The sheriff agreed. "One of the reasons I decided to settle in this town and run for sheriff was because," he half laughed and emphasized his next words, "*murders don't happen in small towns.* Now, at fifty-nine," he lifted the soft drink bottle into the air, "I'm thrust back into the action."

Cruz studied the man, while he took a swig from the bottle. He was heavyset with broad shoulders, sporting a full head of graying hair. His thick and neatly trimmed mustache was dark. His uniform seemed to fit him, despite the extra pounds he had no doubt added since being elected sheriff. Desk jobs had a tendency to create 'spare tires' on even the fittest of people. She watched him remove a pair of wire-rimmed eyeglasses from his shirt pocket and put them on with one hand, while picking up a sheet of paper with the other hand.

"I'm sure I know, but just so we're on the same page, would you mind telling me why you're here?"

Cruz shifted in her chair. "Director Jameson sent us to see if we could be of assistance in your investigation into the dead body that was found earlier today."

Decker looked over the top of his eyeglasses. "How *is* Phillip?"

"He's doing well."

"We go back a few years..." He grinned and added, "...before he became a," Decker tilted his head back and forth, "big-time lawman."

Realizing Sheriff Decker and Director Jameson were friends, and that Decker's words contained no malice, Cruz smiled. She appreciated the man's laid-back personality and welcoming demeanor. The word 'refreshing' came to her mind.

"We met about fifteen years ago. He was a Special Agent back then, looking into a case I was working in another state. He's a good man. That's why I contacted him about this." He looked down at the file. "Well, that and I recognized *you* in the photo. I must admit I didn't expect a visit from you, however. I appreciate you making the trip."

She glanced at Ashford. "Thank you, Sheriff Decker. If we can be of assistance, please let us know. That's what we're here for."

"Where would you like to start? Have you had a chance to go over the information I sent your boss?"

"We have, but I was hoping you'd fill in the gaps, personally."

Decker nodded. "Of course...The body was found in a parked vehicle at a mini mall on Fourth Street, near the William Penn Highway."

Cruz interrupted. "Do you know who the vehicle is registered to?"

"It was reported stolen this morning by the owners, David and Jenny Parker. I sent a deputy to the house and their story checks out."

Cruz nodded. "Who found the body?"

Decker glanced at the paperwork. "It was an employee of the gas station in the same mall. He was on his way to work, saw the car and thought something was wrong. Only the poor fellow's definition of *wrong* was that the person inside the vehicle might need assistance."

"Have you questioned him?" Cruz turned toward Ashford and made a writing motion.

"We have and he's not a suspect. We have an estimated time of death and the kid has a solid alibi. No, he was just in the wrong place and happened to be the first person to see the grizzly sight." Decker went back to his notes. "Authorities were called a little after sunrise and the first deputy was on-scene ten minutes later to secure the area. I arrived an hour after that and came upon the circus. People were milling around, trying to get a better look at the carnage."

Ashford wrote something on the small notepad in his hand. "Yeah, there's nothing like starting your day with a shopping trip and a dead body."

Before Decker could comment, Cruz leaned forward. "Are there any security cameras that might have picked up the vehicle and the person who—"

Decker shook his head and Cruz stopped. "There are two cameras facing the crime scene, but it's too dark to see anything. The two nearest lights in the parking lot were not working—bulbs were burned out. The stolen car was parked between them."

"What about fingerprints?"

"There were plenty of those." Decker removed his eyeglasses and put the end of one bow between his lips, forcing him to speak through clenched teeth. "Problem is they all matched those of the owner and his wife. And, as I said, they have a good alibi." He leaned back in his chair, his eyeglasses coming to rest on his chest. One question had been on his mind all day. "Agent DelaCruz, do you have any idea why your picture was with the body?" He grabbed the photo and pointed toward it. "And, what's with the drawing of the crown and the words 'winner' scribbled on it?"

"Believe me, Sheriff, I wish I knew." Cruz had been racking her brain over the same question, since the meeting in Jameson's office. One answer had repeatedly surfaced in her mind, but she kept dismissing the notion, not wanting to go down that road so soon. She stared at Sheriff Decker. The look in his eyes told her he had been contemplating a similar conclusion. *I guess it's time to float my theory.* She used the armrests to push her body further back against the chair. "It may be too early to say this, but my gut tells me you have the makings of a serial killer on your hands, Sheriff." She reviewed the details in her head. "Most murders don't end with the body in this condition...with pictures attached to it. Those elements have some kind of meaning to the killer."

Sheriff Decker rocked forward in his chair and threw his eyeglasses on the table before grabbing the pop bottle. "I was afraid you were going to say that." He took a drink and returned the bottle to the desk. After swallowing the liquid, he sighed. "I've been thinking the same thing."

Cruz sat erect. "Sheriff, I'd like to take a look at the body. Is there any chance of that happening?"

Decker studied his watch. "The M.E. is going to have his report to me later today." After a few moments, he picked up the phone. "Let me see what I can do."

∞ ∞ ∞ ∞ ∞ ∞ ∞

Chapter 7: Victim

"The victim is a white female around forty years of age. There were no other wounds on the body. The cause of death was..." Dr. Thomas Drake, Huntingdon County Medical Examiner, paused and held out his hand toward the headless body of a woman, lying on the examination table. "Well, you can see for yourself the cause of death."

Special Agent Cruz made the sign of the cross, touching the fingertips of her right hand to her forehead, chest and left and right shoulder. In her mind, she said a prayer for the deceased. This was not the first dead body she had seen; however, seeing the lifeless remains of crime victims always affected her. At times like these, she questioned her decision to go into law enforcement. As soon as the thought entered her mind, she ushered it out. She was meant to be in this profession. It was not easy, but no occupation was.

Dr. Drake, a scrawny and scraggly man in his late thirties, had unkempt light-colored hair. His eyes were narrow slits that rested above a pointed nose and small mouth. His calm and quiet manner seemed befitting of a man in his position. "Fortunately, I can say that she most likely did not suffer. Although I can't verify it, I would have to assume she was struck on the head prior to *it* being separated from her body. The blow alone may have been enough to cause her death. Either way, I don't believe she felt much pain." Whether he knew it or not, Dr. Drake's voice had a soothing effect.

Cruz made a slow lap around the table, searching for anything out of the ordinary. Stopping at the middle of the table, she examined the wrist. The hands of the body had been lopped off as well. *Why would someone cut off the hands?*

Ashford seemed to read her thoughts. "Whoever did this, must not have wanted the identity of the victim to be known." He made a chopping motion with his hand. "Take off the hands and the head and no one can use the fingerprints, face or dental records for identification purposes."

Cruz noticed a small tattoo of a skull on the left shoulder of the body. Instead of crossbones beneath it, there were two straight lines forming an 'X.' Using the camera on her phone, she snapped a picture of the tattoo. She could not place it, but she recognized the image from somewhere. She stowed her cell phone and nodded at Dr. Drake. "I've seen enough." She faced Sheriff Decker. "If you don't mind, Sheriff..." Behind her, Dr. Drake zipped shut the black bag that held the body. "Can you take me to the crime scene?"

... ...

After surveying the parking lot where the body was discovered, Cruz and Ashford spent the next few hours with Sheriff Decker, reading and re-reading reports from deputies, Dr. Drake's autopsy report and individual statements from the man who found the body, and the couple who had their car stolen. Cruz had Ashford send everything to the information analysts at the FBI. At this point, they had no leads to follow.

"Any luck?" Decker had entered the office and was rounding his desk.

Cruz closed the file folder she was perusing and tossed it across his desk. She realized she had been slouching in her chair, resting her crossed ankles on the edge of his desk. She dropped them to the floor and stood. Pointing toward the desk, she said, "Sorry about that."

Decker smiled. "Don't worry about it. I do it all the time." His hands held two plastic cups of coffee. He raised the cups and flicked his eyes back and forth from her to Ashford.

"Thank you." Cruz accepted the cups and gave one to her partner.

Ashford took a couple of sips. "Thanks, Sheriff."

Decker spun his chair around and sat. "Were you folks planning on heading back to D.C. tonight? If you are, you should probably take a look outside." He leaned backward and opened the shades, revealing a blinding snowstorm. Everything was white. "There's almost six inches on the ground and the weatherman says to expect another six in the next few hours. Apparently, we've had snowfall rates exceeding an inch per hour."

Cruz and Ashford had been so focused on the investigation that neither one had taken the time to step outside or near a window. She pivoted her head toward him and arched her eyebrows. Her Dodge Charger was going to have a difficult time in six-plus inches of snow. She did not look forward to the white-knuckle drive home. "Do you think we can make it?"

He analyzed the situation before falling back on his sense of humor. "Sure, we can do it. Go slow, keep both hands on the wheel and we should make the three-hour trip to D.C. in..." he pretended to be doing calculations in his head, "six or seven hours."

Decker stood. "You're both adults, and far be it from me to tell you what to do, but if it were me, I wouldn't attempt it. We've got places where you can hunker down and ride this thing out."

Cruz and Ashford took turns staring at each other and looking out the window.

"Listen, if it makes your decision any easier," Decker jerked his thumb over his shoulder, "I know the owner of a bed and breakfast, the Gateway Mansion, that's just a couple of blocks from here. It's a beautiful building, nice and clean." Sweetening his offer, he added, "I saw where it even got 4.7 stars on Google."

Cruz smiled when she heard the older man reference the search engine giant. He was a good man. His hospitality had been nothing short of warm and friendly, a gracious host. She wished all her interactions with local police could be this amicable.

Decker could see she was mulling over his proposal. He grinned. "Just so you know I've taken the liberty of reserving two rooms at the Mansion."

Cruz chuckled and glanced at Ashford, who wasted no time indicating he was more than happy to spend the night. Coming back to Decker, she smiled. "Thank you, Sheriff. We'll take the rooms. How much do we owe you?"

He plucked his jacket from the back of his chair and swung it around his shoulders. "No charge. It's the least I can do for you coming all this way and lending a hand." He twisted his wrist to see the time. "Come on. If we hurry, I think we can get you two some dinner before they close down the kitchen over there."

∞ ∞ ∞ ∞ ∞ ∞ ∞

Chapter 8: Mansion

January 10th, 7:33 a.m.

Special Agent Cruz scampered out of the bathroom and hurried toward the bed. With one hand holding a towel against her body, she picked up her cell phone with the other hand. She did not recognize the number. "Special Agent DelaCruz," she said. Glancing down, she watched water droplets land on her feet and the plush brown carpeting.

"Special Agent DelaCruz, this is Sheriff Decker. I hope I didn't wake you."

"No, I was just getting out of the shower. I'm putting you on speakerphone. Hold on." She tapped her phone and put it on the bed, so she could use both hands to dry her hair. "What can I do for you, Sheriff?"

"There's been a murder up in Youngstown, Ohio. A headless, handless body was found along the road. I'm on my way to pick you up. How much time do you need?"

Cruz shut her eyes and grimaced. A few seconds later, she opened them. "I'll be out front in fifteen minutes. Thank you, Sheriff."

... ...

Ten minutes later, Cruz holstered her pistol and stuffed her red blazer and slacks into an overnight bag. Having been caught in the field earlier in her career with nothing but the clothes on her back, she always kept extra clothing in her Charger—underwear, pants, shirt, socks and personal grooming items. She had exchanged the red slacks for blue jeans and added a white blouse under her black turtleneck sweater, mostly for warmth. She had no other shoes, so she was wearing the same high heels from yesterday.

She glanced at her phone on the bed. A green light on the device was blinking, indicating she had a new text message. She donned her long black overcoat and secured the buttons before snatching her phone. Halfway through reading the message, someone knocked on the door, but she did not hear the noise. Her jaw dropped and she went back to the beginning of the message.

Ashford knocked on the door to Cruz's room for a third time. "Cruz, are you in there? I got a call from Sheriff Decker. He's waiting for us downstairs." He put his ear to the door. "Cruz, can you hear me?" He rapped on the door with his fist.

Cruz heard the pounding, but the ruckus sounded far away. She pivoted, sloughed toward the door and opened it.

"Good morning." Ashford took a step backward when she brushed past him, never acknowledging his greeting. He watched her move toward the stairs, nose stuck in her phone. *It looks like someone didn't get enough sleep last night.* After she rounded the corner, he turned to shut the door. His eyes spotted her overnight bag on the bed. He started to call out to her, but stopped. Retrieving the bag, he took a quick look inside the bathroom and saw she had forgotten a few personal items. He chucked them into the bag, scanned the main room for additional items and left.

... ...

Cruz exited the bed and breakfast. Her attention was focused on the text message. Two steps past the door and she felt a stiff wind, followed by the sensation of her shoes filling up with cold and wet snow. Breaking away from her phone, she noticed the sidewalk had not been cleared. She waded through several inches of the white stuff on her way to Sheriff Decker's vehicle.

Closing the passenger door, a chill went up her spine when the vehicle's heater made light work of the snow in her shoes, transforming the snow into water. Inwardly, she groaned and made a mental note to add boots to her overnight bag. She whipped her head back and forth, searching for the bag. "I'll be right back. I forgot—" The back door on the driver's side opened and Ashford climbed inside. She rotated her head, saw her bag and nodded at him before sitting straight in her seat. "I'm all set, Sheriff."

... ...

"Is this all you have?" Cruz did not look up from the paperwork in her hands.

Decker pointed. "That's all that came in. They're in the preliminary stages of gathering evidence and getting statements from those who have any information."

Cruz re-read the report, handing each page to Ashford after she was finished with it. Giving the last page to him, she dug out her mobile from the front pocket of her jeans. "How far away is Youngstown from here?" She typed in the town's name on her navigation app.

Decker was faster than the navigation app. "It's three hours to the northwest, just over the Pennsylvania/Ohio border. Are you planning on heading up there?"

She looked beyond his shoulder at the snow-covered trees and vehicles. "I have to." She motioned toward the papers in Ashford's hands and went back to her phone. "This can't be a coincidence. My gut tells me they're connected."

Decker opened a desk drawer. "Well you're going to need these." He held out a set of keys. "They belong to a cruiser out back, a four-wheel drive SUV. In the back—"

Cruz raised her hands and shook her head. "No, I couldn't impose like that. You've been great to us, Sheriff." Her eyes shifted to the wintery mess beyond the window. "I think my vehicle can make the drive." She was trying to convince herself as much as Decker.

Decker spun his head to the left and hailed her partner. "Agent Ashford," he said, before tossing the keys. Ashford barely had time to react, catching the keys in one hand, while using his other hand to keep the paperwork from falling to the floor. "In the back of the vehicle, you'll find a vault. The entry code is written on a sticky note in that file folder. Inside the vault are a pump-action shotgun and an AR-15. Feel free to use them."

Cruz smiled at Decker. "You're not taking 'no' for an answer, are you, Sheriff?"

His head down, he shook it slowly. "The area north of here got hit harder than we did. It snowed all night. They might not even have the interstates cleared yet." He motioned toward his desk. "Leave your car keys, and I'll have one my deputies park your vehicle with my patrol cars. It'll be safe, until you return for it."

"Thank you, Sheriff. I—we really appreciate *everything* you've done for us." She stuck out her hand and Decker shook it.

He maintained his grasp of her hand. "Just do me a favor. When you catch this S.O.B., and something tells me you *will*, I want to hear about it...from *you*." He let go of her hand. "In the meantime, I'd appreciate it if you kept me informed of any progress you make."

Cruz squeezed her fingers into the pocket of her tight-fitting jeans. Her hand emerged with her car keys. "You can count on it."

"If I get any new information, I'll pass it along." Decker got Ashford's attention. "Good luck to you both."

Ashford closed the file and shook Decker's hand. "Thank you, Sheriff. It's been a pleasure working with you."

Decker nodded and replied, "Likewise." He pointed at the keys in Ashford's hand. "Deputy Barnes will escort you to the SUV."

Cruz thanked Sheriff Decker again before following her partner out of the office.

∞ ∞ ∞ ∞ ∞ ∞ ∞

Chapter 9: Text Message

8:44 a.m.
Interstate 99
25 miles north of Huntingdon, Pennsylvania

Ashford stepped on the accelerator and the Ford Explorer's engine roared. Pressing down on the turn signal, he merged onto Interstate 99, near Tyrone, Pennsylvania. Sheriff Decker was right when he said the area to the north had received more snow. The further away from Huntingdon Ashford and Special Agent Cruz got the worse the highway became. Fortunately, many drivers had opted to stay home. Ashford and Cruz were making good time. The forty-five minute drive from Huntingdon to Tyrone had been quiet. Outside of informing him that she wanted to stop at a store that sold boots, Special Agent Cruz had not spoken a word, choosing to stare into her phone the entire trip.

He turned on the radio and found a local station playing classic rock and roll. *Yes, this is a great song.* Singing the song in his head, he drummed on the steering wheel.

Cruz hit the radio knob on the dash, plunging the interior into silence. "If you don't mind, I'm not feeling in the mood for music." She went back to her phone.

"Are you all right, Cruz? Outside of your last sentence, you haven't said two words. Is there something bothering you?"

"I'm fine."

Ashford snorted. "I'm fine. That's usually what I say when I don't feel like talking to people."

Cruz scrolled down the page on her phone. "Then you'll understand when I say 'I don't feel up to talking.'"

Ashford nodded and said, "Except I'm not *people*. I'm your *partner*." His words hung in the air. "You've been acting strange all morning. What's wrong?"

She shut her eyes and let her head hit the headrest. "I'm not sure you can help, Ash. My problem is of the female nature...I think only another woman could understand."

He squirmed in his seat and peered out the window. Bringing his attention back to the road, he adjusted the rear view mirror and cleared his throat. "Okay, I'm an adult." He bobbed his head left and right. "I know how the female body works...Maybe I can help. Talk to me."

Cruz rolled her head to face him. Her face was void of emotion, but she was smiling on the inside. This was the most light-hearted moment she had had, since leaving the Gateway Mansion. "It's not *that* kind of a female problem."

His posture relaxed and he melded into his seat. "Thank God for that."

Cruz grinned, but the fleeting joy drained from her face.

"So, what's got you down?" More silence. After more than a minute of awkward stillness, Ashford sighed. "All right, if you don't want to tell me, that's okay. I'll just sit here and keep—"

"He broke up with me."

Before Ashford could ask the question, his mind, and Cruz, answered it.

"Derek broke up with me this morning...in a text message." She whipped her head around toward Ashford. "He broke up with me *in a text message.*" Her voice grew louder. "Who does that? Who ends a relationship by sending a *freaking* text message?" She raised her hands. "I'm sorry about the language. I'm just so p—...*upset.*"

Ashford held back a snicker. He could have counted on one hand the number of times he had heard her curse, and still have a couple fingers left over. *I'm not sure 'freaking' even counts as a swear word.*

Dropping her phone into her lap, she tapped her chest. "He didn't even have the—" This time, she caught herself. "G*uts* to tell me to my face...or call me," she said, her voice breaking on the last word. She twisted in her seat. "What's wrong with men? They're so quick to fight when they've been dissed, but they can't seem to muster the courage to tell the woman they've been dating for months that it's over."

Let's not throw us all under the bus. He let her remark go. She was speaking from her pain.

"I don't get it." She held up her phone. "I thought we had a great relationship. Can you believe

I was going to take him to meet my mother? What's wrong with me?"

Ashford wanted to answer the question. *There's nothing wrong with you,* however, he kept quiet, thinking she had been right. This was a conversation to be had with another woman. His words may not be well received, considering he was from the same gender that dumped her. The best thing he could do was to listen and not speak, acting as a sounding board.

"What a big mistake that would've been," she stated, pivoting back to her right and crossing her arms over her chest. Her mind was going a hundred miles an hour, thinking back to all the time she and Derek had spent together. *Were the clues there? Did I not see them? How could I be so stupid?* "Never again, Ash...I'm *done* with men." Realizing her overly dramatic statement, she backtracked. "At least I'll never fall for another man like Derek—gone all the time on business trips...suddenly leaving the country for work. No, the next man I date is going to have a nice boring job, or he'll work from home. He'll have a pocket protector, a computer degree and be safe and predictable. I'm through with the *mysterious* and *daring* men."

Ashford eased the Explorer to the right, taking the exit for North High Street, the road that would get them to the next leg of their journey.

Cruz gazed at the distant pine trees, their boughs hanging low from the weight of the wet snow. Her mind drifted back to Christmas, and the ski trip to the Northeast she and Derek had taken. She had no idea how to ski, but she had enjoyed spending time in front of the lodge's fireplace, drinking hot chocolate and watching the skiers glide down the hill.

Seeing the sign for US-322, Cruz blinked her eyes a few times, and she was jolted back to reality. Ashford coughed and she realized he was probably feeling uncomfortable. *I've really dumped a lot on him.* She watched him out of the corner of her eye. *He probably has no clue what to say to me.* Facing her partner, she apologized. "I'm sorry about all this, Ash. I should've just kept it to myself."

He cranked his head toward her and intentionally quieted his voice. "You've got nothing to be sorry about. You've done nothing wrong. I'm your partner and *friend*. I'm there whenever you need me." A split-second later, he smacked the steering wheel with the heel of his hand. "I just wish I could do something. That son of a—" He made a fist and shook it. "If I ever cross paths with him, I'll—"

Cruz grabbed his wrist. "No, you won't." She knew if Ashford did cross paths with Derek, he'd make good on his promises. "You'll leave him alone. I'm a big girl and I'll get over this...*eventually.* I don't need you landing yourself in jail for assault." She felt the power in his arm. "Do you hear me? I don't need saving." A few seconds later, the muscles in his arm relaxed. Letting go of his arm, she settled into her seat.

"Who said anything about saving?" Ashford grumbled. "You know I just like hitting stuff...people." Feeling her disapproving look, he curled up the right side of his mouth to show he was kidding. Ashford flicked his eyes toward her. "Do you want my take on the situation?"

Knowing she was going to get his opinion, regardless of what she said, Cruz extended her open hand in front of her body, giving him the floor.

"I always thought you could do better." He tapped his brakes for a slow-moving vehicle ahead and grunted, "Come on." Passing the car, he recalled their conversation on the way to Huntingdon. "I sound like a broken record, but you're a great gal, Cruz. You already know how I feel about you and what you've accomplished. Any man, who would dump you, is a damn fool. Don't waste any more of your time on him. It's over. See ya...wouldn't want to be ya."

Cruz grinned, her spirits rising. "See ya...wouldn't want to be ya? Did you just make that up?"

"No, I heard it in an old movie I watched last week." He smiled. "It seemed appropriate."

Her giggle built into laughter. "Thanks, Ash. I needed that." Moments passed in silence. "You're a great guy, too. You know that?"

He nodded. "I know. You're a lucky lady to be teamed up with me." He tilted his head, his face deadpan. "But, don't go getting any ideas." With his finger, he made a circular motion toward his body. "This is off limits. We're strictly professionals."

A wide smile formed on her face. "It'll be tough, but I'll try to control myself." She turned on the radio. "I believe someone wanted to listen to a little music." Instead of music coming through the vehicle's speakers, an announcer was rattling off sports scores. She moved her hand to the tuner.

Ashford wrapped his hand around her wrist. "Hold on. The Capitals played the Penguins last night. I want to find out who won." Since moving to Washington, D.C., he had gone all in on Washington teams, especially the Capitals and the Redskins.

"Are those hockey teams?"

He looked at her as if she was from another planet. "Of course they are," he answered before remembering she was a football fan. "Oh, that's right. You're still clinging to the hope the Cowboys will have a winning team again."

Having grown up in Texas, Cruz was a lifelong fan of the Dallas Cowboys. This past season had been brutal. The Cowboys only had two victories, finishing the season at two and fourteen. Recalling both victories and the team they had beaten, she smiled. "Well, at least we seem to have the Redskins figured out."

Bearing the weight of the playful verbal jab, Ashford grabbed his chest as if he had been stabbed with a knife. "Ouch, that hurts." He would have gladly accepted the teasing for the remainder of the drive if it meant keeping her mind off her troubles.

∞ ∞ ∞ ∞ ∞ ∞ ∞

Chapter 10: Youngstown

12:07 p.m.

Clearing the Interstate 80 overpass on Churchill Hubbard Road in Youngstown, Ohio, Ashford and Special Agent Cruz saw the patrol car blocking traffic. He tapped his brakes and eased the SUV to a stop.

A young patrol officer approached, leaned over and put his gloved hand on the door. Puffs of air shot out of his mouth and nostrils when he spoke through the open window. "I'm sorry, but you're going to have to turn around. There's a crime scene up ahead and the road is blocked." He pointed toward the direction from which Ashford and Cruz had come. "If you just head back—"

Ashford opened his FBI billfold. "I'm Special Agent Ashford and," he motioned toward Cruz, "this is my partner. We're *here* for that crime scene."

The officer glimpsed the badge, cocked his head and spotted Cruz's credentials. "All right, you can go on through. It's crowded up there. You're probably going to have to park along the road and hoof it the rest of the way."

Ashford hit the button for the power window. "Thank you, officer. We'll manage." He maneuvered the SUV around the officer's vehicle and accelerated. Coming upon the cadre of emergency vehicles, he pulled to the side of the road and shut off the engine.

Cruz opened the passenger door and stepped into a ten-inch snowdrift. She was grateful for the quick shopping trip to the department store back in Clearfield. Twenty minutes after entering the store, she emerged wearing a black pair of knee boots over her blue jeans. The boots were snug over her calves, while the opening flared enough to keep it from rubbing on the back of her knee. At three inches, the heel was a little higher than she would have preferred, but the chunky block style was much better than a pointed stiletto. Having purchased another pair of socks and adding long underwear under her jeans and sweater, Cruz felt prepared for whatever Mother Nature threw at her.

Slamming the door, she swung her black knee-length overcoat around her shoulders, flipped out her pony from inside the jacket and overlapped the lapels. She scanned the area. To her right were a few homes. The owners had ventured into the road to see the commotion. Across the road was an open field. Farther up the road, on either side of the police vehicles were wooded areas. She trudged through the snow, her right boot sinking deeper into the upward sloping snow bank. Rounding the front of the SUV, she joined Ashford.

He had changed his wardrobe, too, exchanging the dress pants and shoes for jeans and brown six-inch high cross trainers. He kept his suit coat. He may not have been a fashion statement, but he would not be slipping in the snow.

Striding toward the scene, they were stopped by another officer, who let them pass under the yellow crime scene tape after seeing their badges.

Cruz turned back to the officer. "Who's in charge of the investigation?"

He pointed and said, "That would be Detective Brinkman."

Cruz and Ashford headed toward the detective. She reached into her pocket for her identification and hailed him, her voice rising, "Excuse me, Detective Brinkman."

Brinkman kept his head down, writing in a notepad. "You're a long ways from home, aren't you deputy?"

Cruz shot a look toward Ashford.
Deputy? "We're not deputies."

Brinkman pointed with his pen toward their SUV. "Does that mean you stole a patrol vehicle from the Huntingdon County Sheriff's Department?"

Cruz shook her head and removed her hand from her coat pocket. "We're with the FBI."

Brinkman raised his head, squared his shoulders and glared at her. "I suppose you're here to pull that jurisdictional B.S. and take over this case. What kind of a stake does Uncle Sam have in this anyway?"

Cruz breathed deeply and sighed. This interaction with local law enforcement was familiar. Most lieutenants, detectives, sheriffs got upset at the prospect of a case being taken away from them. Throughout the years, she had suspected that many of them did not even want the case to begin with; however, take a case away from them and they would brawl with anyone to keep it.

Detective Brinkman was in his early forties. He had brown hair, tinged with sporadic gray patches. His face was pocked and his nose was crooked, possibly from being broken earlier in life. A bushy mustache covered his upper lip, the ends of the strands curling into his mouth when he spoke. He seemed to be physically fit, but it was difficult to verify through the bulky winter coat he wore.

"No, detective, we're not here to take over your case. We're investigating a murder in Huntingdon. We heard about this one and discovered some similarities." Cruz spotted a black tarp near the tree line. Assuming it was covering the body of the victim, she pointed toward the tarp. "Do you mind if we have a look?"

Brinkman countered with a question of his own. "What similarities?"

Ashford answered. "No head and no hands."

Brinkman grunted. "Do you have any leads on who did it?"

Cruz shook her head. "That's why we drove all this way. This is our only one. Can you tell us if you found anything on the body?"

Brinkman rotated his upper body. "Hey, you," he shouted. When three officers turned to face him, he pointed at one of them and the man ambled over to the detective. Brinkman went back to writing in his notepad. "Show these two the body and give them whatever details we have at this point." Walking away, he grumbled, "I've got important things to do."

Before the officer was within earshot, Ashford smirked. "Ah, yes, Youngstown's finest at work."

"Whoa, hold on." The officer made sure Brinkman was gone. "Don't lump us *all* into *his* category."

Realizing the officer had not been out of earshot, Ashford apologized. "I'm sorry about that."

"I'm Officer Jeffers." He stuck out his hand. Cruz and Ashford shook it. "Some of us still take pride in our work. What can I do for you?"

Cruz motioned with her head. "For starters, I'd like to see the body."

∞ ∞ ∞ ∞ ∞ ∞ ∞

Chapter 11: Body

Officer Jeffers drew back the tarp and revealed the headless and handless body of a black man. "A snow plough driver spotted the body just before sunrise. Unable to stop, he ended up tossing a mound of snow over it. Fortunately, he stopped his truck and called the police. Within thirty minutes, several officers were here. We were able to locate it in no time."

Special Agent Cruz observed the body, made the sign of the cross and closed her eyes. *May God have mercy on your soul and bring peace to your loved ones.* The snow around the body was deep. She had to lift her leg into the air before taking a step.

Jeffers had seen the body, but the sight disgusted him each time he pulled back the tarp. "What kind of sicko would do something like this?"

"What was found on the—" Cruz stepped and sunk in deeper than she expected. The snow rose to within an inch of the top of her boot. Her upper body wobbled.

Jeffers grabbed her flailing arm, keeping her from toppling to the side. "Easy, there," he said. "It's deeper than it looks."

"Thank you, I'm good now." She would have to inspect the body from her current vantage point. "What was found on the body?"

Jeffers gestured toward the naked remains. "As you can see, there were no clothes. The only thing recovered was a picture or photograph of a woman in a bikini."

Cruz gawked at the officer. "Let me guess. There was a crown scribbled above the woman's head, along with the word 'winner' written on it."

Jeffers frowned. "Yeah, how'd you know?"

"Lucky guess," chimed Ashford. "Any chance we could see it?"

"Sure." He waved his hand at the body. "I'll get it for you as soon as we're done here."

For the next few minutes, Cruz bent over, squatted and leaned, trying to glean any shred of evidence she could from the corpse.

Ashford used his camera phone to snap a few pictures of the man's remains from different angles. Not learning from Cruz's exploits, he almost fell on his butt when he stepped into a deep snow bank.

She stood. "I think I'm done here." Struggling to free her feet from the white stuff, she pushed off with her back foot and lunged forward, only to sink further into the snow.

Jeffers locked hands with her, as if they were going to arm wrestle, and pulled. Ashford came from the other side and grabbed her free hand. Once she was standing on manageable drifts, Jeffers let go. "I'll be right back with that picture, ma'am."

Ashford tilted his head toward the body. "What do you think?"

Cruz brushed the snow off her boots and the bottom of her overcoat. Standing, she let out a visible breath of air and rubbed her hands together, drying and warming them. "It has to be our man who did this. The condition of the body is the same as our woman in Huntingdon. The photo will be our lynchpin."

Jeffers returned and held out a plastic bag with a picture inside. "Here you go."

A few seconds later, Cruz and Ashford confirmed it was the same image found with the first victim. She gave the evidence to Jeffers and thanked him for his time. After he had left, she and Ashford made their way to the road. She panned her head from right to left, starting with the restaurant at the edge of the tree line. Beyond the yellow crime scene tape, a few dozen onlookers were blowing into their cupped hands, braving the cold weather to get a glimpse of the brutality.

Ashford followed her gaze and seemed to know what she was thinking. "What is it with people and gore? They don't get enough from television and movies. They need to see it firsthand, up close, live and in person."

"People have become desensitized to violence, Ash. They have to keep upping the dose. Seeing a violent death...as you say, 'up close and in person' certainly accomplishes that."

... ...

Thirty minutes later, Cruz and Ashford had gotten as much information as they were going to get from the officers. Statements from people who may have noticed something and the autopsy report were hours away from being completed. They found

Detective Brinkman, thanked him and headed toward their vehicle.

"I don't know about you, but I'm hungry." Ashford regarded his partner. "What do you say we grab a bite and plan our strategy?"

Cruz's stomach had been growling for the better part of an hour. "Yeah, that sounds good." She glanced over her shoulder and spied the crowd, which had grown in the last half hour. Turning back, she stared at the snow, while she walked. Ashford's words had kept returning to her mind, gnawing at her subconscious.

"What about pizza?" He had his cell phone in hand. "It says there's a joint not too far from here."

She reached the front bumper of the SUV, stopped and whirled around. Squinting, her eyes darted left and right, scrutinizing every face in the crowd.

Ashford broke away from his search and saw the look on her face. He had seen the expression many times. More importantly, he knew what the expression meant. "What's up, Cruz?"

She raised a finger and wagged it at him. "They need to see it firsthand."

"What are you talking about?"

"He's here." She bolted toward the crowd, her unbuttoned overcoat flaring like a cape. Skidding to a halt, she ducked under the yellow tape and took off running again. Seconds later, she came to a stop, standing in front of the mob. The people formed a semi-circle. Her head pivoted left and right and back again. Retrieving her cell phone, she opened the camera and started taking pictures.

Ashford came up behind her. "What are you doing?" Catching his breath, two large clouds of air escaped his mouth. "Talk to me."

Cruz pivoted and touched the phone's screen...*snap*. "The killer...he's here. I can feel it." She rotated her upper body...*snap*. "Some of these serial killers need to return to the scene to see their work *firsthand*." She took several additional pictures before studying the individual faces in the crowd, hoping the killer would somehow magically reveal himself.

"That's a longshot, Cruz." Ashford snapped his head back and forth, not knowing what or whom he was trying to find. "Besides, he's already seen his work."

"Yeah, but he was alone then. Now, he has an audience. Anyway, at this point, *longshots* are all we have." Spinning her head toward the restaurant, her eyes settled on a man. He was watching her. The hairs on the back of her neck stood and she shivered. He was wearing a black ski hat and dark blue puffer coat. Dark sunglasses concealed the upper half of his face. A crooked grin formed on the lower half. The sun, directly behind him, was obscuring her vision. She took a step toward him, but closed her eyes and jerked her head away when the door to the restaurant swung open and the sun's rays reflected off the glass, blinding her. Sticking out her hand to block the sun, she spun her head back toward the man. He was gone. She whipped her head back and forth, trying to spot him. The tingling in her neck traveled south. Despite the cold, she was perspiring. She was certain she had stared into the face of evil.

"Did you see something?" Ashford was standing behind her, staring along her line of sight.

"I don't know...maybe. Do you see a man in a black hat and blue coat...sunglasses?"

Ashford spied the people. "No, I don't." Continuing to study the faces of the bystanders, he motioned toward her phone. "What do we do with those pictures...turn them over to the analysts at the Bureau...see what their facial recognition software comes up with?"

She re-collected herself, shaking her head back and forth and blinking her eyes. She spun around and locked eyes with her partner. "I don't think we have that much time." She took a couple steps toward the SUV, stopped and peeked over her shoulder. "We need to get creative if we're going to catch this guy before he kills again." Cruz tapped the screen on her cell several times. "Sheriff Decker, this is Special Agent DelaCruz. I need your help."

∞ ∞ ∞ ∞ ∞ ∞ ∞

Chapter 12: Starving

2:02 p.m.

"Thank you, Sheriff. I really appreciate this. Please send the files to Agent Ashford's phone." Special Agent Cruz listened. "That's the right number. I'll let you know if we find anything new...thank you." She disconnected the call and stuck out her finger. "He's sending you video footage and several still shots of the parking lot." She took another bite of the pizza slice, dropped the crust onto a paper plate and wiped her fingers with a napkin.

Ashford finished his third slice and cleaned his face and hands before picking up his phone. "I hope you're right about this." He tipped back his soft drink and took three big gulps. "If it doesn't pan out, we're right back to square one."

After leaving the crime scene, Cruz and Ashford had rented a hotel room off Interstate 80 and ordered out for lunch. They had missed breakfast and were starving. The pepperoni, ham and mushroom slices had been greasy, but they filled the void in their stomachs. Cruz knew the food would sit in her belly like a rock; however, a home-cooked meal was not possible under these conditions.

Cruz had contacted Sheriff Decker and asked him to send the video from the crime scene in

Huntingdon. After he had reminded her that the area around the dead body was dark, she told him she wanted the footage from when he had arrived on the scene to when the body had been taken away. Her plan was to examine the people from the crime scenes in Huntingdon and Youngstown, hoping to find someone at both locations. In the last hour, she had studied all the pictures on her phone, committing them to memory. She was especially interested in the one she snapped of the man in the black ski hat and puffer coat. Seeing his face multiple times had made her skin crawl, but she forged ahead.

Ashford's phone sounded. "I just got the files."

"Good. We'll work from here." Cruz stood and cleared the table she had been using for lunch. She crossed the room and dragged a second chair to the table, moving her discarded boots to the side. "What did he send you?" She sat and leaned to her left to get a better view of the videos.

"It looks like I've got two long videos and more than two dozen picture files." He slid his finger across the screen several times.

Cruz brought up the first picture on her phone. "Let's start with the stills. They'll be easier to cross off the list." She held up her finger. "Before we do anything, we should forward all this to someone at the bureau. That way, we'll have more eyes on this than just ours."

... ...

An hour later, Cruz stood and paced back and forth in her stocking feet, one hand on her hip and the fingers of the other rubbing her eyes. After several trips, she stopped, stretched her arms over her head and leaned from side to side. Walking back to the table, she took a couple swigs from her water bottle. Her eyes compared the images on both mobile devices, while she undid her ponytail and let her hair fall. Shaking her head, she ran the fingers of both hands through the long locks, finishing with a vigorous scalp massage. She and Ashford had viewed the pictures and they were fifteen minutes into the first video. So far, they had no matches. *This is taking too long. If the killer was at the second scene, he's getting away and we're losing ground.*

Ashford stood, circled behind her and performed a shortened version of calisthenics, loosening his muscles and getting his blood pumping. "This doesn't look very promising." Hands on his hips, he cranked his head as far as it would go to the left before doing the same thing in the other direction. "I wonder if the techies in Washington have had better luck."

Cruz brought up the images from Ashford's phone. Starting with the first one, she scrolled through them one at a time. Her finger hovering in the air, she paused, gawking at an image. Leaning over her chair, she picked up her phone, tapped the screen a few times and whipped her index finger over the device's surface, until she found what she wanted. Throwing her hair over her left shoulder, she grabbed both mobiles and held them up side by side. She squinted and her eyebrows scrunched together.

Ashford stood beside her. "What's up?"

"Here, take this." She gave him his phone, while bringing hers closer to her face. "Do you see the man in the black coat in the center of your screen?"

Ashford zeroed in on the man and replied, "Yeah."

She put her phone next to his and pointed out a man on it. "What do you think?"

Ashford spun his head left and right several times, comparing the two men. He motioned with his head. "This one is a profile shot, but I definitely see a resemblance. How'd we miss it?"

In her mind, Cruz knew the answer. She had been so focused on finding the man in the black ski hat and dark blue puffer coat she had lost a certain amount of objectivity. She chastised herself for the rookie mistake, but took solace in knowing she was not the only one who made the error. She forfeited her cell to Ashford. "Contact the D.C. computer gurus and have them run this man through facial software. All other cases can wait, until they get him identified. When they do, I want everything on him, *including* the kitchen sink."

He nodded and brought up the number for the FBI in Washington.

... ...

Twenty minutes later, Cruz eyed her partner, her ears straining to hear his conversation.

"This is Ashford." He gave her the 'thumbs up' sign. "Uh-huh...uh-huh...okay, send it all to me ASAP."

After Ashford had finished the call, Cruz peppered him questions. "What is it? What did they find? Were they able to ID him?"

"It turns out the guy was already in the criminal database. His ex-wife had filed for and received a restraining order against him a few years back. She claimed he had been stalking her and she was in fear for her life. A little while later, he violated the conditions of the order."

"So, who is he? Where is he?"

Ashford stuck his finger in the air. "Hold on, Cruz." He grinned. "You can only get so much information over the phone. The agent I spoke with said he was sending me—" a chime sounded and he checked his mobile. "Okay, our man's name is Harold Hawkins. He's a thirty-five-year-old computer information engineer for a Fortune 500 software company out of...scratch that...he *was* a computer information engineer. He was fired three years ago. It looks like it happened right around the same time as his divorce and the restraining order."

Cruz stepped into one of her boots, bent over and ran the zipper the length of the shaft. "So, do we have someone with anger issues or mental health problems on our hands?" Her voice low, she was thinking aloud rather than speaking to her partner. "Has he finally snapped after all this time and gone on a killing spree?"

"He and his wife lived in Chelsea, near Boston, while they were married. No kids in the picture from what I can see here."

Cruz sat on the edge of the bed and leaned forward to grab her second boot. "Where is he living now?" She jammed her foot into the boot, crossed the leg over her knee and slid the zipper to the top. Remaining in the cross-legged position, she drew her hair back and formed a ponytail. "Do we have a last known address?"

Ashford scrolled down the document. "According to his last tax return, he's living in an apartment in Cleveland."

Cruz stood and grabbed her overcoat. "Cleveland's not that far from here."

Ashford did a quick Google search. "It's less than two hours away."

She scanned the hotel room for personal belongings. "Okay, if you're ready, let's go."

∞ ∞ ∞ ∞ ∞ ∞ ∞

Chapter 13: Fire

4:04 p.m.

Slamming the front door, he dropped his bag onto the rug and peeled away the winter coat and stocking hat. The drive from Ohio had taken longer than he had expected. Traffic had been horrible. He remarked to himself, "For people who live in this part of the country, you'd think they'd know how to drive in the snow." Walking further into the living room, he noticed the atmosphere had a cold bite to it. Passing by the couch, he opened the glass doors on the fireplace and began the process of building a fire.

Twenty minutes later, a fire was blazing behind the closed glass doors. Undersized for the cabin, the fireplace was the only source of heat. The propane tank in the backyard was empty and there had not been enough time to schedule a delivery. He would have to take whatever heat the small fireplace provided. Ambling toward an end table, he turned on a lamp. The incandescent bulb cast a sparse yellow tint over everything and everyone.

He stood behind the couch for several minutes, his mind recalling every detail of what he had done. The woman had been difficult. Holding the bat, an aluminum softball bat, his hands trembled. He had been a good ball player when he was younger. Hitting the ball was his favorite part of the game. He loved the feeling that radiated from the bat through his hands and arms when he hit the ball on the bat's sweet spot. That same feeling came rushing back to him when he struck the woman on the back of the head, sending her to the kitchen floor, but not before her head bounced off the kitchen table. She was most likely dead before he went to work on her with the other tool in his duffle bag.

The big black man had been easier. Having experienced the taking of human life once already, he found the act surprisingly routine the second time. Unfortunately, the second victim had not expired from the blow to the head. He was alive when the axe was pulled from the bag.

The man leaned over the couch and gently touched the cheek of a young blonde-haired woman. She flinched and drew away from his hand. He pursued her, until she could withdraw no further. Stroking her hair, he curled up the corner of his mouth. "Don't worry. It won't be long now. I have something special planned for you." He played with her hair for a few minutes, much like a cat toying with a mouse. "First, I need some sleep, however. Be a dear and keep quiet, will you?" He patted her head and sloughed into the bedroom.

∞ ∞ ∞ ∞ ∞ ∞ ∞

Chapter 14: Cleveland Heights

4:55 p.m.

The address for Harold Hawkins was a three-story red brick apartment building near the intersection of Overlook Road and Euclid Heights Boulevard in Cleveland Heights, Ohio, an inner-ring suburb of Cleveland. Agent Ashford parked the SUV in front of the building on the opposite side of the street. He and Special Agent Cruz got out of their vehicle and jogged across the lane, Ashford sticking out his hand to stop an oncoming car. They ascended the concrete steps and entered the structure.

Cruz approached a man behind a short counter. She glimpsed his nametag—Paul Kentwood, Manager. He was barely out of his teens. His skinny frame was hunched over the counter. Pimples dotted his facial landscape, though he did a good job of masking them. He greeted her in a professional tone, befitting that of a more mature man.

"Good afternoon. How may I help you?" He stood and pushed aside the magazine he had been reading. Standing, he easily surpassed Ashford's height.

She displayed a digital copy of a search warrant she had obtained during the trip from Youngstown. Finding a judge on a Sunday afternoon to issue the warrant had been a challenge. Luckily, her colleagues in D.C. had done most of the work. "I'm Special Agent DelaCruz of the FBI and I have a search warrant for the apartment of Harold Hawkins."

The manager's eyes moved from the phone in her hand to Ashford's FBI badge. Unsure what to say, he shrugged. "What do you need me to do?"

She verified the man's name. "Mister...Kentwood, do you have a key to his room?" When he nodded, she opened her hand. "Give it to me." He complied. "Where's his room?"

The manager pointed through the ceiling. "It's on the top floor, last one on the left."

Cruz stuffed the room key and her phone into her coat pocket. "Are the rooms near his occupied?"

Thinking, Kentwood rolled his eyes. "There are three other apartments on the floor...and two of them have tenants."

She headed for the stairs, beckoning him to follow. Once the trio was on the third floor, she whispered to the manager, "I want you to quietly knock on the doors of these other two apartments and get them to open the door. Tell them whatever you have to. Just get them to open up."

He gently knocked on the first door to his right. When a voice from the other side answered, he said, "This is the building manager. I...you have a delivery downstairs." He shot a look toward Cruz, who nodded her head. "You have to sign for it."

The door opened and Cruz stepped in front of Kentwood.

Presenting her credentials, she motioned for the man to undo the chain latch and open the door. "I'm with the FBI. Are you alone?" The man nodded. "I need you to quietly exit your room and go downstairs."

... ...

Once both apartments were cleared and she had sent the manager away, Cruz pulled back the right lapel of her overcoat and drew her pistol. Ashford did the same. She pressed her back against the wall. Hawkins's apartment door was to her left. Standing on the other side, Ashford confirmed he was ready. She beat on the door with her fist. "Harold Hawkins, this is the FBI. We have a warrant to search the premises. Open the door, *now*." There was no response. She repeated the command. Not getting an answer, she slid the room key into the doorknob and unlocked the door before moving the key toward the deadbolt.

Ashford gripped his pistol with both hands and shifted his weight from one foot to the other, rocking in place. "What's the hold up, Cruz?"

She fiddled with the key for a few seconds. "It won't work. It's not the right key."

"I'll get the manager." He took two steps toward the stairs.

"Forget it." She moved aside and tilted her head toward the door. "This is what you live for. Have at it."

Ashford's face transformed into that of a kid on Christmas morning. Holstering his weapon, he backed against the apartment door on the opposite side of the hallway, squatted and charged, ramming his shoulder into the door. The door buckled, but did not yield. He made a second run and it bowed in further.

Cruz watched her partner rub his shoulder, while he prepared for a third attempt. "I thought you said you played *linebacker* in college."

"They moved me to running back during the preseason."

Making ready to storm the apartment, Cruz smiled. "I'm beginning to understand why."

"Watch it," he shot back, his face contorted. He lowered his center of gravity and bolted forward.

The short screws securing the deadbolt to the doorframe were no match for Ashford's third try. The wood fibers surrounding the screws split apart, sending tiny slivers into the dwelling. Cruz spun around and rushed inside, her partner a step behind, pistol in both hands.

Everything in the studio apartment could be seen at once. A kitchen and dining area was at the far end. A combination couch and bed was in the center. A flat-screen television was mounted on the wall to her left. Cruz moved left and peeked around the corner to the bathroom. Retreating, she said, "Clear."

"Clear," said Ashford.

Cruz holstered her weapon and double backed toward a small end table under the television. She picked up a stack of unopened envelopes, addressed to the apartment's occupant. "Okay, let's *turn* this place."

... ...

Cruz looked at her phone. The time read 6:13. She and Ashford had spent more than an hour combing every square inch of the apartment. They found nothing out of the ordinary, nothing that pointed toward the possibility that Harold Hawkins had anything to do with the murders. He had run up his credit cards and had little money in the bank; however, that only made him an average American, not a serial killer. She walked to the couch and hauled off the cushions before probing the sides and back with her fingers.

Ashford inspected the built-in wall closet for the third time, sliding suits, shirts and sweaters along the metal bar supporting the hangers. He started to turn around, but stopped when he noticed a panel at the back of the closet. It did not match the pattern of the adjacent paneling. Spreading his arms, he pushed the clothing out of the way. He poked the nonmatching section. It curved inward. Under his breath, he said, "What the hell?"

Down on all fours and peeking under the couch, Cruz heard him. "What is it?"

"I'm not sure." He slipped his fingers behind the panel. He pushed, pulled and slid, until it separated from the rest of the wall. His eyes grew wide. "Uh, Cruz, you better have a look at this."

She had been standing beside him when he lowered the panel. "Oh, my..." She saw a three-foot-by-three-foot white poster board filled with pictures, mostly of her. Her stomach churned, while her heart slowly crept into her throat. Shifting her eyes left and right, up and down, she thought she was seeing a scrapbook of her life. The board held newspaper clippings from ten years ago when she competed at the Miss America Pageant, a photo from when she received special recognition from the FBI for arresting the Mexican drug trafficker and several pictures from when she was with the Dalhart Police Department. A copy of the same image found on the murder victims was positioned in the center of the board.

Ashford was the first to notice the most disturbing part. He pointed and cranked his head toward her. He watched her jaw drop and her eyes bulge.

Cruz's cheeks and forehead turned red and she squinted. Clamping her jaw shut, she clenched her fists. The fingernails dug into her palms. If Hawkins were standing in front of her, she would have ended his life—no handcuffs, no Mirandizing, no judgment by a jury of peers. No, a single bullet would have accomplished all three.

At the end of Ashford's pointing finger were pictures of Cruz, and her boyfriend (ex-boyfriend), at her home in Maryland. One picture featured her in a pair of shorts and a tank top, mowing the lawn. Another photo showed her and Derek kissing at the front bumper of his Mercedes. A third image had been taken at a restaurant. Sitting cross-legged at a café table, she was depicted reading a newspaper; however, the focal point of the snapshot was her above-the-knee skirt, legs and high heels. Several additional photos of her at different locations, wearing similar outfits, littered the right side of the board.

Cruz forced herself to open her hands, flexing her fingers several times. *Cool it, Raychel. This isn't helping. You'll get this son-of-a...breathe...just breathe.* She let out a slow breath and focused on the other half of the poster board.

Ashford backed away. "Well, we certainly have our man. How do you want to play this?" She did not answer him. "Cruz, you okay?" Realizing the stupidity of his question, he gave her a moment.

Cruz was sweating. The top portion of her long underwear was clinging to her body. Pinching her sweater and long underwear between her fingers, she fanned herself. The anger inside continued to rise and fall, despite her self-counseling. Her mind went back to those moments portrayed on the board and she put a hand to her stomach, suppressing the urge to vomit. She now had a glimpse into what it must feel like to be a victim of a robbery. No, being stalked was worse. A robbery was a moment in time. As devastating as it was, being robbed was a singular event. Being stalked was something that continued for days and months, even years. She flicked her eyes to the right. Even though this man had not physically touched her, he had violated her in other ways. She dropped her head, shaking it back and forth.

Ashford put a gentle hand on his partner's shoulder. His voice barely audible, he said, "What do you want to do, Raychel?"

Raychel. He only used her first name when they were off the clock, having a beer, hanging out. This was not one of those times. There was work to be done. *It's time you get your head on straight, Raychel.* Slamming her eyes shut and scrunching up her face, she asked for help. *God, grant me the serenity to accept the things I cannot change, courage to change the things I can and the wisdom to know the difference.* Seconds later, her eyes opened, she lifted her head and issued commands. "Get a BOLO" —*Be On the Lookout*— "on this guy. If he's spotted, no one is to engage...monitor only. I want to know when he's found ASAP. I repeat...*no one* moves in on him."

Ashford nodded. "You got it."

"Contact Jameson and have him move Heaven and earth to get every scrap of digital data on *Mr. Hawkins*. I want his credit cards tracked, his cell phone tapped. If he has a Facebook page or a Twitter account, I want to know if he makes a post, sends a tweet or if he scratches his...*all of it.*"

Ashford retrieved his cell phone and walked away.

Cruz rested her crossed arms on her chest, studying the board. Shifting her weight to her right foot, she rocked her left boot backward, balancing on the heel. Cocking her head to the left, her eyes zeroed in on a picture. She plucked the image from the board and drew it closer. A black man and two white women, dressed in eveningwear, were shown. The man had his arms around the women. All three were posing for the cameraperson. She walked to the floor lamp.

Ashford returned. "I issued the BOLO and got Jameson—"

Cruz spun. "Take a look at this." She pointed at the left shoulder of the woman on the right before pulling out her phone.

Ashford seized the picture.

She found the snapshot of the tattoo on the left shoulder of the first victim. Both of them moved their heads back and forth, comparing the images.

"It looks the same," he said.

Cruz pointed. "I know her. She used to be a member of an all-girl band. They had a hit single a decade ago." She put her finger over her lips. "What was their—"

"Oh, yeah, the Red Roses," Ashford blurted. "I remember that." The rhythm of the song played inside his head. His lips moved, while his mind tried to sing the words. He saw Cruz out of the corner of his eye and stopped miming. She was grinning. His defenses kicked in and he felt his ears getting hot. "What?"

"I always thought you were a rock and roll kind of guy. I never figured you for an *all-girl groupie.*"

The redness in his ears moved to his cheeks. "I was a dumb teenager." He shrugged. "What did I know?" He motioned toward the picture, eager to get her back on track. "What's this got to do with our killer?"

Cruz tapped her phone's screen, until she had the information she wanted. "Jaclyn

Doherty...drummer for the band, the Red Roses...thirty-nine-years-old...fits the age of our first victim." After scrolling the page, she snapped her fingers and twisted her hand to show her discovery.

Ashford pursed his lips. "That's it all right. It's a perfect match."

Cruz had found the logo for the Red Roses, a skull with a pair of crossed drumsticks beneath it. The same skull and drumsticks on the body of victim number one.

"So, now we know *who* she was, but that doesn't tell us *why* she was targeted."

Cruz took the picture from Ashford. There was something else familiar about it, but she could not place it.

He waved his arm toward the closet. "And, why is she on this board...with all these pictures of you. How is she connected to *you?*"

Ashford's words echoed in her mind...*Connected to you...me.* She let her head fall backward. "Of course," she said, eyeing the snapshot and validating her theory. She spun on the heels of her boots to face him. "I know who the third victim is going to be."

∞ ∞ ∞ ∞ ∞ ∞ ∞

Chapter 15: Gulfstream

7:19 p.m.

With Ashford listening, Special Agent Cruz had called Director Jameson and informed him of the killer's next target. The two women and one black man in the picture from the poster board had been the three judges for the Miss America Pageant for the year Cruz had competed. With one of the three judges confirmed dead and a second one reported missing, Cruz urged Jameson to focus all efforts on locating the third judge, Mandy Mason.

Officers from the local police department were dispatched to Mason's home in Syracuse, New York. After getting no response, they entered the home and discovered signs a struggle had taken place in the living room. The rest of the rooms were neat and tidy. After interviewing neighbors, family members and friends, it had been determined the thirty-one-year-old aspiring singer and actor had not been seen or heard from in three days. Her phone had been turned off and/or the battery had been removed, not allowing the device to be tracked.

Unable to find Harold Hawkins through his digital footprint, Cruz and Ashford turned their investigation toward the ex-wife, hoping to interview her and get information that might lead to Hawkins's whereabouts.

Ashford tucked his phone into his jacket pocket and got the attention of his partner, who was speaking with one of four FBI agents from the crime lab. Hawkins's apartment had been turned over to them and they were gathering potential evidence for analysis.

Cruz wrapped up her conversation with the agent and joined Ashford near the sofa bed. She folded her hands and touched her lips. "What is it?"

Ashford grinned. "Are you praying for good news?"

She chuckled. "Have you got some?"

He nodded. "Hawkins's ex-wife, Brenda Dobson, is still living in Chelsea, the same home they shared when they were married."

Cruz's rolled her eyes and her shoulders slumped. "I thought you said you had *good* news." After a moment of reflection, she shook her head. "I can't do it, Ash. I'm not driving that far." She produced her mobile. "That's got to be eight or nine hours away."

He clarified the distance. "It's nine hours and thirty-four minutes."

She scrolled her contact list and tapped the screen. Twenty seconds later, she heard a man's gruff and raspy voice on the other end of the line.

"This is Special Agent Smith." Anthony Smith was the Special Agent in Charge of the FBI Cleveland field office. He and Cruz had known each other, since her training days at the FBI academy.

Assisting in training the cadets, he was the first person to notice her raw skills and potential as an agent.

"Hello, Anthony. It's Raychel...Special Agent Cruz."

A split-second went by, while Smith attached the name to the face. His smile came through the phone. "Special Agent Cruz, it's nice to hear your voice. How've you been, Raychel? It's been a long time, since we've talked."

"Yes, I've been busy lately."

"Are you still working with that knucklehead?"

She shifted her eyes toward Ashford. "Yes, *Curtis* is standing here with me."

Having heard Smith's comment, Ashford let out a short laugh. The two knew each other well. Ashford tried to get Cruz to relay a message to his friend. "Tell him, he can kiss my—"

She waved her partner off before covering her ear with her hand. "I'm afraid this isn't a social call, Anthony. I'm in the middle of a case and I need a favor from you."

After chuckling over the implication of Ashford's partial sentence, Smith grew serious. "Name it, Raychel, and you've got it. What can I do for you?"

... ...

Checking the time on her phone—8:31 p.m., Cruz eased the seat back aboard the Gulfstream V. Having taken off from Cleveland-Hopkins International Airport, she and Ashford were flying to Boston to interview Hawkins's ex-wife. Special Agent Smith had the jet standing by when Cruz and

Ashford arrived. The aircraft left the runway fifteen minutes later. Smith had informed her that a car would be waiting for them when they landed at Boston Logan International Airport. The driver had instructions to take them wherever they needed to go.

Cruz leaned back and let the muscles of her body relax. Doing the math in her head, she concluded she had spent a little over six hours in the SUV. Add the time she had expended on raiding Hawkins's apartment, investigating a crime scene, staring at photos and figuring out Hawkins's twisted scrapbook of her life, and she felt as if she had been awake for twenty-four hours straight. The flight to Boston would take a little more than an hour. Since there was nothing she could do in that time, she planned to get some rest.

Tucking the pillow behind her head and raising the blanket to her chest, she closed her eyes. At first, the day's events rushed to greet her mind. Playing like a movie, she saw the mangled bodies of the murder victims, the faces of the people trying to get a peek at the gore, the photos of her in Hawkins's apartment. Even Derek, her boyfriend, skipped past her subconscious. She corrected herself. *Ex-boyfriend, Raychel...he's your ex-boyfriend. Get over him. Move on.* That was going to be easier said than done. She had invested much of herself into their relationship. Erasing him from her life would not be a simple task. She breathed deeply and let the oxygen gently escape her drawn lips. No more than ten minutes eclipsed and she was asleep.

∞ ∞ ∞ ∞ ∞ ∞ ∞

Chapter 16: Chelsea

9:57 p.m.

After the Gulfstream V touched down in Boston, Special Agent Cruz and Ashford hopped into a waiting Chevy Tahoe and made the short drive north to Chelsea to a neighborhood on Hawthorne Street. She noticed the lack of snow on the streets. The wintery weather had bypassed Boston and the surrounding area. Although the temperatures were warmer, compared to Ohio and Pennsylvania, she was glad to have her knee boots and long underwear. A fierce wind was blowing from the north, dropping the 'feels like' temperature ten to fifteen degrees.

The driver of the SUV, a young agent in his mid-twenties, found an open parking spot a block away from their destination. Cruz and Ashford exited the vehicle and strode along the sidewalk. They came to a three-story brick building with a white picket fence next to wooden steps that led to the front door. The red brick building was connected to several other multi-level dwellings, creating a massive structure.

Ashford knocked on the door. The porch light came on before the curtain covering the small window in the door moved slightly. The owner had been expecting the federal agents. The door opened and Brenda Dobson appeared in the doorway, barefoot and dressed in pink sweatpants and a black sweatshirt. Feeling the rush of cold air, she folded her arms and hunched her shoulders.

Cruz presented her identification and said, "Brenda Dobson?" When the woman nodded, she motioned toward her partner. "Ms. Dobson, this is Special Agent Ashford and I'm Special Agent DelaCruz of the FBI. We're here to speak with you about your ex-husband. You should have been expecting us."

Brenda forced a smile. "Yes, of course. Please come in."

Once the agents entered the house, the threesome headed for the living room. Cruz and Brenda sat on a black leather couch, while Ashford stood next to Cruz, his eyes scanning the room.

The living room was small. The usual furnishings—couch, reclining chair, coffee and end tables, were close together. The light brown walls were barren, except for a couple of paintings. Against the wall in front of the couch was a tiny entertainment center, which supported a small flat-screen television.

"Is there anything I can get you...water, coffee?" Brenda said, starting to stand.

Cruz shook her head. "No thank you." Her words stopped the young woman. "We're sorry it's so late, Ms. Dobson, but it's very important that we talk to you about your ex-husband."

Brenda coerced another smile. Her lips parted, briefly showing a set of straight and white teeth. Bright blue eyes popped outward above her round and full cheeks. She had long blonde hair, parted on the side. Wavy bangs fell across her forehead, covering her eyebrows. Her cute physical appearance added innocence to her pleasant and charming demeanor.

Cruz regarded the woman's features. *How does someone like her end up with a monster like Harold Hawkins?*

"Please call me Brenda."

"Thank you, Brenda." Cruz spent a few minutes sharing as many of the details as she could regarding the murders. Her next words took the sweet girl by surprise. "Brenda, we believe your ex-husband is involved in these killings."

Brenda leaned backward. Her warm and friendly face became stoic and her body grew tense, rigid. *Harold...a murderer?* She lowered her gaze and stammered, "I...I don't know what to say."

Cruz put her hand on Brenda's arm. The woman flinched at the touch. "Is there anything you can tell us that might help find him?"

"I don't know. He was always a little odd. I mean...he's a computer person...a little geeky. I can't believe he's capable of doing something like this."

Ashford stuck his fingers into the front pockets of his jeans. "You filed a restraining order against him. Did you feel threatened? Did you think he was going to hurt you?"

Brenda tilted her head to observe the man towering above her. "I got that because he had become paranoid during our divorce. He was spying on me at all hours of the day and night. I was scared.

He thought I'd been cheating on him and I think he was trying to prove it."

"Were you?" Ashford stated, flatly. He watched Brenda's upper body rock backward. At the same time, Cruz shot him a menacing look and he regretted his words. He was operating on instinct, questioning the woman as if she was a suspect. He backtracked. "I'm sorry, ma'am. I didn't mean to accuse you of any wrongdoing."

Cruz covered for her partner. "It's been a long day. Please excuse us. We've been on the go, since early this morning." After a short pause, she continued. "Do you know where your ex-husband might be? Does he have relatives or friends in the area or another state? Is there property somewhere where he might be staying? Anything you can remember would be helpful, Brenda."

Shaking her head, Brenda stood and walked toward the entertainment center, her hands folded over her mouth. "It's been such a long time since I've seen or spoken with him. Our divorce was *not* amicable. When it was finalized, I wanted nothing to do with him. I just wanted to move on with my life."

The face of Cruz's ex-boyfriend flashed across her mind. "I can certainly understand that. And, I'm sorry to have to make you relive bad memories; however, a young woman's life is at stake. Again, any scrap of information you can remember that might lead us to your ex-husband..." Cruz let her voice trail off, waiting for the woman to respond.

Her back to Cruz and gazing at the floor, Brenda shook her head. "Nothing's coming to mind. I wish I could help you. I really do."

Cruz stood and fished out a business card from her pocket. It was late and the woman was tired. Pushing her to think of something was not producing results. "Thank you for your time. If you remember *anything*—"

Brenda whirled around and stuck her finger into the air. "Wait a minute." She stared past Cruz's shoulder. "Harold spoke about a piece of property...that had been in his family for decades."

Cruz glanced at Ashford. He was already fishing for his pen and pad of paper.

Brenda rolled her eyes toward the ceiling, while gently tapping her nose with her fingertips. "He always talked about taking me to *the cabin*...but he never did. After all these years, I just forgot about it." She shrugged. "To tell you the truth, I have no idea if it ever existed."

Cruz stepped forward and put her hand on Brenda's upper arm. "Do you know where the property is located?"

Several moments went by, while Brenda recalled her ex-husband's words from many years ago. "I think he said it was lakefront property in...upstate New York...Albany...or Utica..." She brought her shoulders to her neck and contorted her face. "I'm not sure. I wish I knew more."

Cruz rubbed the woman's arm and smiled. "You've given us a place to start." She faced

Ashford. "Find out if Hawkins, or anyone in his family, owns property in New York."

"I'm on it." He pulled out his phone and left the room.

She focused on Brenda. "Can you remember anything else he might have mentioned about this cabin?"

∞ ∞ ∞ ∞ ∞ ∞ ∞

Chapter 17: Full Circle

January 11th, 1:07 a.m.
New York

Wearing an FBI bulletproof vest over his dress shirt, Ashford adjusted the sling on his MP5 rifle, chambered in nine millimeter. His mind drifted back to the apprehension of Peterson and Lopez. "It's funny how it all comes full circle to a *cabin in the woods.*"

Using the sliver of information from Brenda Dobson, the information analysts in Washington, D.C. had discovered a tract of land south of Northville, New York on the eastern shore of the Great Sacandaga Lake, deeded to Harold Hawkins's great grandfather. Off County Road 109 and surrounded by a mini forest, a single-story fifteen hundred square foot cabin sat on the land. Aerial reconnaissance had shown a vehicle parked in the driveway. At the request of the FBI, New York State Troopers were sent to the location. When they checked the license plates, they determined the vehicle had been stolen a day earlier. Upon learning that, Special Agent Cruz decided she had enough information to warrant a visit to the property.

Half an hour later, two Bell 407 helicopters, bound for Northville, lifted off with two FBI SWAT teams aboard. Special Agent Cruz and Ashford were in one helicopter with three SWAT team members, while the second aircraft transported the remaining five members. When the helicopters landed in a deserted field a mile south of the cabin, two SUV's from the New York State Police were waiting to drive them the rest of the way.

Standing at the rear of one of the SUV's, a few hundred yards south of the cabin, Cruz had discarded her overcoat and put on a bulletproof vest over her black sweater. She double-checked her pistol and holstered it before grabbing an MP5 and making it ready. Letting the weapon hang from its sling, she addressed one of the state troopers. "Both ends of this road have been blocked?"

"Yes, ma'am," replied the trooper, a black man around thirty years old, who was at least six inches taller than Cruz and twice as wide. "As per your instructions, we've evacuated everyone from the three houses north and the lone house south of the dwelling in question. There's no one but us," he pivoted his head, "for five hundred yards in all directions."

Cruz nodded. "Thank you, Trooper Williams...excellent work." She faced the SWAT team leader. "Are your men in position?"

"I've got two men stationed at the back of the structure and one each at the north and south ends. All of them are just inside the tree line. They have orders to engage only if the subject escapes."

"Good. What about the assault teams?"

"Bravo team is standing by near the back door, out of sight and waiting for orders." He gestured toward the man standing behind him. "Phillips and I are Alpha team and we'll be going in the front door," he pointed at her, "with you."

Cruz jutted her chin toward Ashford. "What do our eyes in the sky tell us?" The FBI office in Albany, New York had been monitoring an aerial drone, equipped with night and infrared vision. The drone was hovering high above the cabin.

Ashford held up his hand. "Eagle Eye, this is Agent Ashford. Give me an update." Eagle Eye was the codename for the agent controlling the drone.

"No change, Agent Ashford," said Eagle Eye. "The two heat signatures have not moved since the last update—over."

"Copy that." Ashford eyed Cruz. "There's no change. We still have one signature at the back of the structure and a second one in the middle."

Cruz thanked her partner before turning around and staring in the general direction of the cabin. She rolled her shoulders. Her muscles were tense and her stomach churned at the prospect of seeing action. She thought of the work Hawkins had done on the first two murder victims, leaving behind grisly corpses. The presence of two heat signatures was a good sign. If the third victim was with him, that meant she was alive. Cruz's instincts were telling her to rush the cabin and get to the victim as soon as possible to save her life; however, speed was not always the best course of action. A bull rush sometimes resulted in getting the hostage killed.

That's not going to happen. She was planning her course of action when the SWAT team leader spoke.

"Special Agent DelaCruz, I'd like to advise you to let my men conduct this raid. No offense, ma'am, but we're specially trained for these situations. We can storm the place and have it cleared in seconds."

She rotated her head and saw him out of the corner of her eye. *Bull Rush*, she thought before returning her attention toward the cabin. "Thank you. Your advisement is duly noted."

Ashford stood alongside her. "So, what's going through your head? Do we *storm the place*...sneak in...negotiate with Hawkins? Talk to me."

She placed her hands on her hips. "My gut tells me to go in hard and fast, but we don't know the mental stability of this guy. He could kill her as soon as the door is kicked in. We don't know if Hawkins is even in there. For all we know, two kids could have stolen that car and are hiding out after a joyride."

"We could call in a hostage negotiator...find out if he's in there."

Cruz shook her head. "No, the time for that was when we were in the air. I'm not waiting any longer. Whatever we do, we're doing it *now*."

"Okay, it's your call, Cruz. I'll stand behind whatever you decide."

A full minute passed before she unslung her rifle, placed it inside the SUV and loosened the first strap on her vest.

... ...

Nearly shouting at his partner, Ashford said, "What? Are you crazy?" He turned away. "I've changed my mind. I can't get behind you on this." Spinning around to face her, he thrust his finger toward the cabin. "You'll be in there with a serial killer, *unarmed.*"

The SWAT team leader agreed with Ashford's assessment. "I really must advise against this, ma'am. This course of action is way outside of normal protocol for these situations."

Ashford jerked his thumb toward the man. "You heard him. This is outside of protocol. Or, in layman's terms, this...is...*nuts.*"

Cruz placed her pistol next to the MP5 and removed her vest. "Ash, this whole investigation has been outside of protocol, beginning with a photo of," she poked her chest with her thumb, "*me* in a bikini...to dismembered bodies...to some sick 'this is your life in pictures, Raychel DelaCruz' poster board in an apartment." She put her foot on the bumper of the SUV and touched the top of the shaft of her left boot. "To me, using this guy's twisted affections for me *against him* falls into that *outside of protocol* category. If I can get him to let down his guard, we can take him out before he kills again."

Ashford pleaded. "At least keep the vest on."

"No, I want him to trust me. I want him to see me as the person on his board. Hopefully, he'll open up to me and we'll get a shot at stopping him." She slipped a communication device into her ear and spoke to the team leader. "Get your snipers in position and wait for my order."

He shook his head and sighed. "Yes ma'am."

Placing her hand on Ashford's shoulder, she reassured him. "I'll be fine, Ash. If anything goes wrong," she smiled, "I know you'll have my back."

... ...

Cruz shivered, feeling the cold night air rush under her overcoat. With each step, the snow crunched under the soles of her knee boots. Winter was in full force in this part of the state. She looked to the sky and saw the full moon. There were no clouds to hide it. No clouds also meant the earth was losing the warmth of the day. The thought sent another shudder through her body. Perhaps, the shudder was from what she was about to do. Reaching the beginning of the driveway, where the property opened into a clearing, Cruz heard radio chatter in her ear.

"This is sniper one. I'm in position, awaiting orders—over."

"Sniper two is in position, standing by—over."

Cruz neared the middle of the front lawn. Her heart was pounding in her chest and her pulse had increased. *Is this a mistake? What if I'm wrong and he kills her anyway?* She felt the weight and burden of leadership. It was easier to follow someone else's orders. Being in charge brought with it a heavy feeling of doubt. She could not imagine what Director Jameson faced on a daily basis. *Should we have just stormed the cabin and rolled the dice?* She shook her head to clear away the self-doubt and cobwebs. *You can do this, Raychel. Trust your gut.* Stopping in the middle of the front yard, she held the megaphone to her mouth and pressed the button. "Harold Hawkins, this is Raychel DelaCruz. Don't shoot. I just want to talk."

... ...

Harold Hawkins flipped over, his body propped on his elbows. He blinked and rubbed his eyes. Throwing the covers off, he swung his legs over the side of the bed. Was the voice real or was he dreaming? Rotating his head from side to side, he strained to hear into the silence of the night.

"Harold Hawkins, are you in there? This is Raychel DelaCruz of the FBI. I only want to talk, Harold."

Hawkins jumped from the bed, scrambling to get his pants around his waist. He grabbed the pistol on the nightstand, ran out of the bedroom, crossed the living room and slid to a stop at the front door. Down on one knee, he pulled back the window curtain a fraction of an inch.

... ...

"All teams, I've got movement on the east side, front window."

"Sniper one has eyes, but no joy on the shot—over."

"Copy that. Stand by."

Hearing the chatter, Cruz focused on the front window and spotted the drawn curtain. She raised the megaphone. "Harold, this is Raychel DelaCruz. Can we talk?"

Hawkins stood and darted to the center of the room. He pointed the pistol at the woman lying on the couch and touched the trigger. He heard the voice of Special Agent Cruz through the megaphone. He turned and paced.

The terrified woman was on her left side with her hands behind her back. Her hands and ankles were bound. A strip of duct tape covered her mouth. Her eyes were wide open, watching her kidnapper pace in front of her. She saw her life flash before her eyes when he pointed the gun at her face. Each time he turned away from her, she struggled against her restraints.

Hawkins passed by her, his arms crossed above his head, his gun pointed toward the ceiling. "No, no, no, this was not supposed to happen." He stopped. *I can't believe she's here.* He had spent much time fantasizing about meeting her, and she was standing *outside the door*. He paced. "But, it wasn't supposed to happen this way." He had envisioned meeting her under different circumstances. *This is all wrong.*

... ...

"Come to the door, Harold. Talk to me." Cruz waited, but no one came to the door. "Harold, I'm coming in. I'm unarmed. I just want to talk to you." She heard Ashford's panic-stricken voice in her ear.

"Negative, Cruz, negative. Stick to the plan. Get him to open the door."

Dropping the megaphone, Cruz stepped toward the front door. "He's not coming out and we're losing the upper hand. The longer this goes on the more time we give him to think through his options. He needs to know he's *out* of options. I'm going in.

All teams stand down." She heard the team leader's voice.

"All teams, be advised. We have one confirmed friendly and one possible friendly in the structure...all team members respond."

A chorus of 'copy that' sounded in Cruz's ear. She stopped at the door and extended her hand. Twisting the doorknob, the muscles in her back convulsed and she was keenly aware of a nearby presence. A prayer from her childhood raced to the forefront of her consciousness. She let the words slip past her lips, whispering, "St. Michael the Archangel, defend us in the day of battle. Be our safeguard against..."

... ...

Hawkins stood behind the door, watching it move inward, his gun pointed at the leading edge. The side profile of the woman he was obsessed with came into view. Her slim figure cleared the door and his eyes scanned the length of her body. "Don't move. Don't turnaround. Stay where you are." He eased the door back to its closed position before pressing the muzzle against the back of Cruz's head. "Hands," he ordered. When she stretched out her arms, he searched for weapons on her body. Not finding any, he circled around her and backpedaled, heading for the couch and the woman lying on it. Never taking his eyes off Cruz, he grabbed a handful of the woman's hair and yanked, forcing her into a sitting position. Tears flowed down the woman's cheeks. He moved around the couch and went to one knee, pointing the gun at the base of the woman's skull.

Cruz held out her open hands. "Please, Harold, you don't have to do that. I'm here. We can talk this through. She has nothing to do with this."

Hawkins jabbed the gun toward Cruz. "Shut up! You know damn well this has *everything* to do with her."

Cruz flinched and took a step backward.

He put the gun back against the woman's head. "I'm sorry. I shouldn't have yelled at you like that." He wrenched the woman's head backward, until it hit the back of the couch. Pressing his lips to her ear, he said, "Stop...your crying." Her knees up and her feet hovering, she whimpered behind the duct tape.

For the first time, Cruz got a good look at Hawkins's latest victim. The woman was bound and gagged, naked and trembling, shivering. In the dim light of a single lamp, Cruz could not be certain, but she thought the woman's skin had a bluish tint. Her eyes scanning the room, she felt the absence of heat in the cabin. The inside temperature was not much warmer than the outside temperature. Her eyes went back to the woman. *The poor thing...she must be freezing.*

"You shouldn't be here. You weren't supposed to see this." Hawkins moved the muzzle around to the woman's ear. "You would have found out when it was over."

Cruz squinted at him, grinding her teeth, while her right hand moved a fraction of an inch toward her pistol before she remembered she had left it behind. Seeing the naked woman, Cruz saw the pictures of herself in shorts, skirts, dresses. *Did he ever see me naked? Did he ever peek through a window and catch me undressing?* Revenge resurfaced in her heart. *So many lives shattered...so much pain and misery. He needs to pay.*

Standing, he used his weapon in place of his finger. "*You* should have been Miss America. You know that?" He jammed the gun into the woman's stomach. "She and the others took that away from you."

Cruz focused on his finger, resting on the gun's trigger. *I need to calm this guy down before he twitches.* She willed herself to smile. "Is that what this is about, Harold?" She took a couple steps to her left. "I'm okay with the results of that contest."

"What're you doing? Stay where you are." He squatted behind the woman.

Cruz held up her hands. "I'm just going to sit down." With her right hand in the air, she used her other hand to spin around a straight-back chair. "I'm just sitting down." Holding her hands in front of her chest, she sat. "Second place is not that bad. You don't have to—"

"Why are you here?" Hawkins stood. "How did you find me?"

Cruz crossed her left leg over her right knee. "You left a trail of bodies, Harold. It was only a matter of time before someone followed the trail."

"There's no way you could have identified them."

She crossed her hands over her left knee. "There's always a way."

He shook his head. "No, there's no way. I was careful."

"You got sloppy." Cruz slipped the fingertips of her right hand inside the opening of her left boot, her left hand concealing the movement. "You hung around at both crime scenes long enough to be caught on camera."

Hawkins gazed at a distant corner of the room. His mind connected the dots and he glared at Cruz, his nostrils flaring. "You've been in my apartment, haven't you? You invaded my privacy." He lifted his gun hand toward her. "How could you do that?"

She raised her hands. "Take it easy, Harold. That's my job...I find people who don't want to be found."

"You're like all the rest." His voice boomed. "I thought you were *different.*" He punctuated his words by thrusting the gun toward Cruz. "I thought we could've had something together...once I got rid of that boyfriend of yours."

Cruz arched her eyebrows. *He was planning to kill Derek.* She heard Ashford in her ear.

"He's losing control. This is going south. All teams move in."

Hawkins screamed at her, spittle shooting from the corner of his mouth. "I thought I could *trust* you."

Cruz brought her left hand to her ear. "Belay that order. All teams stand down."

"Who are you talking to?" He spun his head left and right toward the windows, while ducking behind the victim. He shouted. "*Who* are you talking to? Who's with you?"

Cruz lowered her hands. "It's over, Harold. There are two FBI SWAT teams outside. They've got the house surrounded. New York State Troopers are backing them up." She leaned forward. "There's nowhere to run." She studied her adversary. His eyes were wide and his skin was glistening. *Ash is right. He's losing control.* "No one else has to die, Harold." She slipped her hand into her left boot. *Just take a step to your right you son-of—*

Hawkins squinted and wiped the sweat from his forehead with his forearm, never releasing his grip on the woman's hair. He locked eyes with Cruz. "No, you're wrong. One more person needs to die." He let go of the woman's hair and stood behind her, pointing his weapon at her head.

Cruz drew a quick breath and shouted, "NO."

... ...

At the end of the driveway, Curtis Ashford sat in the passenger's seat of the SUV. Cruz's shriek sent his heart into his throat, paralyzing him with fear. The gunshots that followed jolted him back to reality. He pounded on the dashboard. "Go—Go—Go." The driver stepped on the accelerator and the vehicle lunged forward, fishtailing as the wheels struggled to find traction on the snow-covered path. Ashford's mind envisioned the worst. He hated himself for letting his partner go ahead with this stupid plan. *I should've stopped her.* He reached for the door release. Before the vehicle had come to a complete stop, he threw open the door and took off on a dead run toward the cabin. Three feet from the opening to the structure, he launched his body. The cabin door flew inward and bounced off the interior wall, swinging back at him. He took a few awkward steps, stopped and assumed a firing stance with his MP5, his eyes shifting left and right. Two SWAT members rushed in behind him, once more sending the door crashing into the wall. One man moved left, while the other went right, searching for Hawkins. Ashford's eyes settled on the couch and the two women on it. A split-second later, he brought a walkie-talkie to his mouth and yelled into the device, "This is Agent Ashford. Get those emergency vehicles up here *now.*"

... ...
Thirty seconds earlier...

Hawkins squinted and wiped the sweat from his forehead with his forearm, never releasing his grip on the woman's hair. He locked eyes with Cruz. "No, you're wrong. One more person needs to die." He let go of the woman's hair and stood behind her, pointing his weapon at her head.

Cruz drew a quick breath and shouted, "NO." Drawing her hand from her boot, she leveled her Glock 27 at Hawkins. Closing her left eye, she aligned the pistol's sights with his right eye. She pressed the trigger, but stopped when she saw Hawkins put his gun to his right temple. She reapplied pressure to the trigger. *Oh, no, you don't.*

You don't get the easy way out. You're mine. She was a hair short of completing the stroke when she swung her pistol to the left. The report of the weapon sounded in her ears with each successive tug on the trigger.

Lowering the gun, she sprinted forward and kicked Hawkins's firearm away from him. Slipping her pistol back into her left boot, she produced a pair of handcuffs and dropped to her right knee, driving it into his back. Hawkins's cries filled the room when she jerked his arms behind his back and clasped the steel manacles around his wrists. His right hand showed signs of trauma. At the last second, Cruz had opted not to take his life. She shot his hand, forcing him to drop his weapon before he could commit suicide.

Cruz hurried around the couch. She flipped open her knife and the bound woman reeled backward. "It's okay. I'm just going to free you. It's okay." After cutting the ropes, she wiggled out of her overcoat and wrapped it around the woman's naked and shivering body. She carefully peeled back the duct tape from the woman's mouth before sitting and cradling her. "It's okay, sweetheart. You're safe now. He can't hurt you anymore. You're safe." Cruz shook in unison with every tremble and twitch from the sobbing victim's body.

The woman recoiled when the front door swung open and Ashford charged in with his rifle. Cruz held her tighter and stroked her hair. The SWAT members rushed past the couch. "It's okay. It's okay. They're with me. They're the good guys.

You're safe. I promise." She kissed the top of the woman's head before shifting her eyes to the right and giving Ashford the 'thumbs up' sign.

Ashford brought a walkie-talkie to his mouth and yelled into the device, "This is Agent Ashford. Get those emergency vehicles up here *now.*" He ran out the door and returned with a wool blanket from the SUV. He approached the couch and gently covered the victim with the garment before staring at his partner.

Cruz caught his gaze and flashed him a reassuring smile. "I'm fine."

∞ ∞ ∞ ∞ ∞ ∞ ∞

Chapter 18: Cathedral

March 20th, 12:23 p.m.
Washington, D.C.

Special Agent Cruz smoothed her knee-length red skirt, periodically pinching pieces of fuzz from the material and letting them fall to the floor. Her legs would not be confined to pants on this beautiful day. The temperature was sixty-one degrees, on its way to the lower seventies by late afternoon. Abundant sunshine had been forecasted to accompany the unusually warm temperatures. Sitting cross-legged in a chair, Cruz extended her top leg and examined the color of her skin. She chuckled. *You gals need some time in the sun.* The truth was her mixed heritage—her father was of Mexican descent and her mother was Caucasian—gave her tan-colored skin all year long. At the end of spring, the tone darkened and remained that way for the summer. She felt her hip vibrate. Checking her mobile, she smiled when she saw the face attached to the text message from Curtis Ashford. She had not spoken with him, since shortly after starting her new position with the FBI.

Since apprehending Harold Hawkins, Cruz and Ashford had taken on several cases, including exposing a corrupt Washington government official, who later resigned his position. That case led to

Cruz being promoted to a supervisory special agent position in the Fraud and Public Corruption Division. She and Ashford went separate ways. He continued investigating cases, while she sat behind a desk, shuffling papers and clicking a mouse.

Her workload was grueling and boring at the same time. Trading a bulletproof vest for a comfortable chair and an oak desk, she lasted less than two months before walking into Director Jameson's office and resigning from her supervisory role. She wanted to get back into the field. Paper cuts were not her strong suit. Scrapes, scuffs and bruises from arresting criminals were what she had in mind when she became an FBI agent.

Jameson, however, was not going to let a top agent go so easily. Following a fifteen-minute conversation, the two of them reached an agreement and he tore in half her resignation. She would keep her supervisory position and work cases, while Jameson assigned to her a full-time assistant to handle the mundane tasks. Being partnered with Ashford was her only other condition. Jameson quickly agreed. That was Friday.

Today, Sunday, she had gone to Mass and was waiting to meet with Father Pat McMurray. After the meeting, she had plans to spend the day in the park, reading and taking in the sunshine. Her schedule had kept her indoors for weeks and she needed to get outside. The door opened and she cranked her head to see Father McMurray enter his office at St. Matthew's Cathedral in Washington, D.C.

In his late sixties, Father McMurray was tall and lean. His face was long, but filled-out. His hair was gray and he had a bald patch that ran down the middle of his head all the way to the back, stopping an inch above his shirt collar. He closed the door and walked toward his visitor. "I'm sorry it took so long, but I was stopped by Mrs. Holloway. God bless her, but a conversation with her..." He laughed. "Well, let's just say that if you've ever spoken with her, you'll know never to complain about the *length* of my homilies."

Standing, Cruz joined in his laughter and met him halfway between her chair and the one in front of his desk. "I *have* spoken with her. She's a sweetheart, but I agree with you. She can talk your ear off."

Father McMurray took Cruz's hands and kissed her on the cheek. He had met her shortly after she moved to D.C. area. The two became instant friends. Her bright and cheery personality never failed to lift his spirits. He cherished their conversations and the occasional visit. Sitting in the chair closest to his desk, he got comfortable and crossed his legs. "I can't tell you how good it is to see you, Raychel. How've you been?"

Cruz bobbed her head and averted her gaze. "I've been good, Father. And you?"

Father McMurray was a priest by trade, but he had spent three years in college, studying psychology. He was not a licensed psychologist, but his schooling had never left him. He noticed the subtle cues in Cruz's body language. "Life's been very good to me. I can't complain; however, I get the sense you've got something on your mind."

Cruz grinned. He always got to the point. She admired that quality in him. He said what was on his mind. There were no games. "That's why I came to see you. I had a case a couple of months back and...it's been bothering me. Well, not so much the case as my attitude during the investigation."

Father McMurray uncrossed his legs and leaned forward. Resting his forearms on his knees, he listened, while Cruz spent the next few minutes recanting the story of the serial killer.

... ...

"...he took a step backward, Father, but his weapon was still pointed at the woman's head." Cruz made a gun with her right hand. "I had a clear shot, so I put my finger to the trigger. I was determined he wasn't going to take another life."

Father McMurray nodded.

"All of a sudden, he puts the gun to his head and I'm thinking he's going to kill himself." Diverting her gaze, Cruz paused and shook her head, re-living the scene in her mind. "I don't know what came over me, but I felt a rage inside like I've *never* felt before."

"Why were you angry?"

Staring at the floor, reflecting on the question, she felt her pulse beating faster. She locked eyes with him. "After all he had done," she growled, "the people he had killed, the lives he had ruined," she hesitated, "he shouldn't have been allowed to take the *easy* way out. I wanted him to pay...with his life.

And, I wanted to be the one to exact payment. I wanted justice." She backtracked. "I wanted *revenge—*"

Father McMurray held up his hand. "Before you go any further, is this something we should be discussing within the sacrament of reconciliation? Are you here for confession, Raychel?"

Cruz pinched the bridge of her nose and calmed herself. She managed a half-hearted laugh. "I probably should be, Father, but not for this."

He nodded and waited for her to continue.

"As I said, my finger was on the trigger, and I'm ready to drop him." She took a deep breath and exhaled. "I'm not sure what happened next. I think I heard a voice in my head...or maybe I just remembered the words from the bible..." she shook her head slowly. "Anyway, as plain as day," she motioned toward the empty space between them, "just as you and I are talking right now, I hear the words...*Vengeance is Mine.*"

Father McMurray's eyebrows arched and he cocked his head.

"A split-second later, I moved my sights to the left and fired several shots toward his hand, the one holding the gun. He couldn't get a shot off and the weapon fell to the floor." Cruz motioned with her hands. "I rushed forward, kicked the gun away and arrested him."

"And, the victim," said Father McMurray, leaning forward. "Is she okay?"

"She sustained some minor injuries and bruising, but she's expected to make a full recovery."

He resumed his relaxed posture. "Thank God."

Cruz echoed his sentiment. "Everything ended well, Father, but I've spent the last two months thinking about my actions, my *deep desire* to take someone's life. Once he turned the weapon on himself, I knew he wasn't planning to kill the victim. I knew she was safe. There was no reason for me to shoot him. However...knowing he was going to take his own life...I guess you could say I felt cheated. I wanted to be the one to do that." She leaned back and smirked. "I don't know why I didn't just let him pull the trigger. He certainly had it coming."

"But, you didn't." Father McMurray stood, crossed his arms over his chest and held his chin in his hand. He circled behind his chair, staring at the floor. "Raychel, I've known you long enough to know that you're a good person." He wagged his finger at her. "Anyone in your situation could have had the same reaction. You said it yourself. You were tired, under an extreme amount of stress, staring at the source of so much pain and misery. It's understandable to have feelings of anger and want to seek an outlet for it...to seek revenge." He came around to the front of his chair.

Cruz sat straight. "Are speaking as a spiritual counselor or as a psychologist, Father?"

He smiled. "You're getting the best of both worlds, my dear." Sitting, he continued. "The most important thing to take away from this experience is that you didn't allow your emotions to control you. Everyone gets angry. Everyone wants to act out." He tapped the bible on the table to his left. "Even Jesus got angry when he saw His Father's house being used as a marketplace. He overturned tables and chased away merchants."

Cruz's facial expression softened when she remembered the bible passage.

"There was an injustice happening and Jesus was passionate about correcting it." Father McMurray poked his finger in her direction. "You, too, saw an injustice taking place. You felt passionate about correcting it...or in your case, stopping the man from hurting anyone else. In the end, you chose justice over revenge. You chose not to take a life. Instead, you saved," he held up two fingers, "*two* lives."

Cruz cocked her head.

"You saved the victim *and* the criminal's life."

She nodded, gaining new insight into the situation. "What about the 'vengeance is mine' part?"

Father McMurray shrugged. "Those words could've come to you based on your familiarity with scripture. There are several bible passages referencing vengeance. You just said you wanted revenge for everything this man had done." He held out his hands and feigned a juggling act. "Vengeance...revenge...they're the same thing." He tapped his chest with his forefinger. "It's also entirely possible that God's voice was speaking to you, your *heart.*" He placed an elbow on the armrest and massaged his temple with his fingertips. "Do you want my personal take?" He did not wait for an answer. "I think you realized it wasn't your place to pass judgment on another human being, no matter what that person's offenses may have been. No, you faithfully executed your duties as an FBI agent. You served our justice system by arresting the criminal and you served God by saving an innocent life."

Cruz's body sunk into the chair, the weight of her burden fading away. She pondered his words...*serving justice...serving God...saving innocent life*. Her chest rose when she inhaled and held a deep breath of oxygen. Seconds later, she expelled it through her nose and smiled. "Thank you, Father. I feel much better."

Father McMurray stood and met Cruz halfway between their chairs. "You're very welcome. I'm glad I could help."

Cruz hugged the priest. Letting him go, she chuckled. "Hopefully, the next time we talk it won't be such a heavy topic." He laughed and the two strolled toward the door, chatting. Coming to the door, he turned toward her.

"It was good to see you again, Raychel."

"Same here, Father," she replied.

"Take care of yourself." He placed his hands on her upper arms. His voice serene as if he was blessing her, he said, "May God give you His peace."

... ...

Cruz spent a few minutes inside St. Matthew's Cathedral praying before stepping into the sunshine of a beautiful day. Bounding down the concrete steps, her spirit renewed, she fished her mobile from her pocket. "Hey Ash, it's Cruz. I got your text. What's up?"

"You sound in a good mood, Cruuu—" he caught himself. "So, what am I supposed to call you now that you're a supervisor and all...boss...Special Agent DelaCruz...ma'am?"

She chuckled. "Well, I know one thing for sure. I don't *ever* want to hear the word *ma'am*. I'm only four years older than you, not forty." She reached the top of the next flight of steps. "As far as I'm concerned, we're still partners. Call me Cruz. Now, what's up?" She grabbed the handrail and propelled herself along the sidewalk, heading for her car.

"Make sure you keep your chipper attitude, because..."

Cruz ran her fingers through her hair. Distracted, she did not notice the two men approaching and crossed in front of the second man, clipping him with her shoulder. "Excuse me. I'm so sorry," she said, spinning her head back and forth, but never looking directly at him. She went back to her conversation with Ashford and strode away. "I'm sorry, Ash. I missed what you said. I just bumped into someone." Over her shoulder, she heard the man apologize.

"It's my fault, ma'am. I wasn't paying attention."

Cruz closed her eyes. *Ma'am. It's starting already.*

The stranger watched her, hoping to get a glimpse of her face, but she never turned around.

"Come on, Hardy. Let's go," said the man's companion. "We're burning daylight."

Cruz left the sidewalk, crossed the street and got into her Dodge Charger. "Okay, Ash, I'm on my way." She set her phone in the vehicle's center console and picked up the book she was going to read this afternoon. Leaning against the door and peering out the window, she let the sun's rays warm her face. Closing her eyes, she absorbed as much sun as she could. Tossing the book onto the passenger's seat, she sighed and said, "Duty calls."

∞ ∞ ∞ ∞ ∞ ∞ ∞

Email me at alexjander555@gmail.com to receive notifications of new releases and sneak peeks at upcoming books. *Your personal information will never be shared with anyone.*

Thank You

Thank you for purchasing and reading Vengeance Is Mine. My intent with this book was to give readers of my Aaron Hardy series a deeper look into the character of Special Agent Raychel Elisa DelaCruz. Through six books in that series, her role has grown more important. My hope is that readers have made a connection with her and want to know more about her character. Making her the protagonist in this book has allowed me to show more aspects of her personality and draw readers closer to her.

If you liked Vengeance Is Mine, please take the time to visit your favorite bookseller and leave a review. *Reviews are extremely important to authors.* Your comments help us understand what our readers are thinking and feeling about our work. Your review also helps others in the purchasing process. More purchases means others are enjoying our work and want us to write more books. Your thoughts are critical to our success and the availability of good fiction.

I hope you are looking forward to the next book in the series, <u>Defense of Innocents</u>. For a sneak peek, keep reading.

Sincerely,
Alex J. Ander

Other books by Alex Ander:

Aaron Hardy Patriotic Thrillers:
The Unsanctioned Patriot (Book #1)
American Influence (Book #2)
Deadly Assignment (Book #3)
Patriot Assassin (Book #4)
The Nemesis Protocol (Book #5)
Necessary Means (Book #6)
Foreign Soil (Book #7)

Special Agent Cruz Crime Dramas:
Vengeance Is Mine (Book #1)
Defense of Innocents (Book #2)
Plea for Justice (Book #3)

Standalone:
The President's Man: Aaron Hardy Omnibus 1-3
The President's Man 2: Aaron Hardy Omnibus 4-6
Special Agent Cruz Crime Series
The First Agents

Defense of Innocents

By
Alex Ander

Continue reading for a preview
of the next book in the Special Agent Cruz
series...

Chapter 1: Go—Go—Go!

"If we keep to the starboard side and come in from the rear, we should be invisible. Brooks, I want you to lead Bravo Team. Enter the aircraft here through the rear-most door." Resting her foot on the front bumper of a black Chevy Tahoe, Special Agent Cruz leaned forward. Spread out on the hood of the vehicle was a drawing of a Boeing jet. She tapped a spot on the diagram. "Once you've gained entry, separate into two teams. One team clears the rear section, while the second team moves forward. When the plane is secure, I want all members of your team to stack up outside first class and wait for my order. You'll have one minute to get into position. *No one* breaches, until I give the command. Is that understood?"

"Roger that, ma'am," affirmed Brooks.

"The rest of us will comprise Alpha Team. Once we cross under the belly of the airplane, we'll ascend the stairs here," Cruz pointed at the map, "and hold position near the cockpit." She trained her finger on two men. "You and you hang back and secure both staircases." She twisted her torso. "You two are with Agent Ashford and me." The men nodded their assent.

Cruz removed her foot from the bumper and stood on the tarmac. Not wanting to spook the man they were preparing to apprehend, she had chosen to wear her street clothes—knee boots, jeans, sweater and overcoat. The two, four-man SWAT teams were dressed in black tactical gear.

Ashford had an FBI bulletproof vest over his street clothes. "I wish you'd reconsider and," he tucked his thumb under the vest and tugged, "put one of these under your sweater."

She shook her head. "I don't want him to see my bulging sweater and suspect something's wrong."

"He might just think you're a chunky gal and you could get away with it."

The other agents snickered.

She knew there was no malice in Ashford's comment, but she took the opportunity to send a playful shot across her partner's bow, backhanding him in the arm. "You'll regret that when this is over." Turning to the SWAT team members, she cautioned them. "Focus people. The target is highly skilled and trained by our very own U.S. Government. He's had three go-arounds in Iraq and Afghanistan, including the provinces of Helmand and Kandahar. I don't need to remind you those were deadly regions for our troops. After that, he appears to have become a ghost, suggesting Uncle Sam may have tapped him for more...*specialized*...missions." Cruz eyed each man. "Make no mistake, gentlemen. Our man needs no weapon. He *is* a weapon. Take nothing for granted and stay on high alert at all times."

One by one, the SWAT team members responded, "Yes, ma'am."

"Remember," she tapped her chest, "I'm the one who makes first contact. No one does anything without my order." She looked at Ashford and lifted her eyebrows. He pursed his lips and shook his head. She went back to the SWAT team. "This operation should be over in less than three minutes from the time our boots hit the ground. The mobile stairs are already in place, so let's mount up and move out."

... ...

Cruz, Ashford and the SWAT team members stood in a line, stacked near the cockpit door, waiting for Bravo Team to get into position. She stole a glance beyond the opening that led to first class. She spotted her mark, sitting halfway back on the port side of the plane, her right. The flight attendant zipped by him. He leaned toward his window. Cruz looked further back when the blonde attendant slithered between the two drapes. She thought she had seen the helmet of one of the men from the second half of Bravo Team racing up the aisle. Lowering her gaze, she saw her target had returned to an upright position and was staring at her. *Crap!* She slowly leaned back behind concealment. *Did he make us?* Her earpiece crackled.

"Alpha, this is Bravo. We are in position, awaiting your order—over."

When the attendant was safely out of the way, Cruz would give the command; however, the woman never came into view. A few seconds passed. She heard a scuffle, followed by a muffled scream, and she leaned out again. The assailant had one arm enfolded around the attendant's neck, choking her, while pressing the handle of a silver spoon against her throat. He had not drawn blood, but the utensil was deep into the woman's neck. Cruz tapped her earpiece. "We've been made. All teams 'GO.' I repeat...Go—Go—Go!"

∞ ∞ ∞ ∞ ∞ ∞ ∞

Chapter 2: Townhouse

March 20th, 1:32 p.m.
Vienna, Virginia
Two Days Earlier

FBI Special Agent Raychel Elisa DelaCruz climbed out of her black Dodge Charger and closed the door. She arched her back, cupping it in her hands. The forty-five minute drive from St. Matthew's Cathedral in Washington, D.C. had been frustrating. The day was gorgeous and it seemed everyone living between D.C. and Vienna had decided to enjoy the unseasonably warm temperatures and abundant sunshine by taking a Sunday afternoon drive. She leaned left and right, stretching her muscles. Standing straight, she tilted her head backward, closed her eyes and let the sun's rays warm her face. A few seconds later, she heard a low whistle followed by a familiar voice.

"So, this is how you dress when you're off the clock. You look nice, Cruz. I take it this is your Sunday best?" Those close to Special Agent DelaCruz called her Cruz, a shortened version of her name given to her when she was in the military. Her fellow soldiers had joked that her full name was too difficult to pronounce.

Cruz opened her eyes to see her partner, Special Agent Curtis Ashford, standing in front of the Charger. He was dressed in a black suit, white shirt and black dress shoes. His red tie with blue diagonal pinstripes was held in place by a gold tie bar. With the sun behind him, his facial features were obscured in a shadowy blanket. She did not need the sun to see he was smiling. She knew by his tone of voice.

Ashford stood six-feet tall and weighed two hundred pounds. His black hair, dark eyes and long eyelashes gave him a hardened, yet attractive appearance. The square jaw and perpetual stubble on his cheeks took his 'bad boy' good looks to a higher level. He had an athletic frame with wide shoulders, a narrow waist and heavily muscled arms and legs. A football player in college, he made the team as a linebacker. A few practices later, his coaches moved him to running back, where he ran over and through defenders on his way to a school rushing record in his first year. A knee injury in the playoffs ended his college career and derailed his professional football hopes.

Drawing her long and dark brown hair into a mid-rise ponytail, Cruz glanced at her clothes. She wore a matching red suit coat and knee-length pencil skirt that hugged every curve of her well-toned five-foot, eight-inch figure. Below her bare legs, she had on a pair of two-inch high-heel red pumps. A white button-up blouse completed her outfit. She secured the ponytail and smiled. "You could say that." She pointed her chin toward the dwelling Ashford had exited. "So, what do we have here?"

Ashford pivoted and led the way into the 1,200 square-foot townhouse at the end of Oakdale Woods Court. Hardwood floors throughout the structure with crown molding and a private rear patio, the $400,000 home had two levels with spacious bedrooms, two baths and plenty of attic space for storage. The residence was beautiful by any standard. The owners had good taste and good jobs to afford the luxurious amenities.

Ashford and Cruz passed through the living room and entered the kitchen where the first body, a lump covered by a white sheet, lay between the kitchen table and the entryway into the living room. A red streak ran from the edge of the sheet toward the living room. The kitchen was neat and tidy. One spoon lay on the floor near the refrigerator, its door slightly ajar. All the chairs were pushed under the table, except for one. The back of that chair was against the counter halfway between the sink and the refrigerator.

Ashford got the attention of a man standing near the body and made introductions. "Detective Reynolds, this is Special Agent DelaCruz." He motioned toward the detective and glanced at Cruz. "This is Detective Reynolds. He's in charge of the investigation."

Reynolds shook Cruz's hand. "Thank you for coming, Agent DelaCruz." He flicked his eyes toward Ashford. "As I said to your partner, from the looks of what we've got here, we sure could use the resources the FBI can bring to bear in this case." He paused and studied the white sheet. "I haven't seen anything like it in my ten years as a detective."

Short, pudgy and standing three inches shy of Cruz's height, Detective Mark Reynolds was forty-two years old. Brown hair covered his round head. The beginnings of a receding hairline testified to his age. Deep horizontal lines showed on his forehead. Below the lines, thick and bushy eyebrows rested above deeply set eyes. When he spoke, his nostrils flared and the dark mustache under his wide nose moved up and down.

Cruz stepped away from the detective and sat on her haunches in front of the victim. She lifted the sheet. Lifeless eyes stared back at her. She took special note of the multiple gunshot wounds before shutting her eyes and lowering her head. *Lord, grant him peace and eternal rest. In Jesus' name, I pray. Amen.* She gave the man's body another onceover and eased the sheet to the floor with both hands.

Ashford had been hovering over her. "Did you notice the GSW's?"

Knowing the lingo for gunshot wounds, Cruz concurred, "Two to the body...one to the head."

"Do you think it's a coincidence?"

She glanced over her shoulder at the ransacked living room. "Well, if this wasn't a home invasion, then someone went to a lot of trouble to make it look that way."

Ashford poked a finger at the sheet. "Thugs don't shoot like that."

Her knees together, Cruz pushed on them and stood. Adjusting her skirt, she mulled her partner's words.

Reynolds agreed. "The wife's body is upstairs and has the same pattern—double tapped in the chest and a single shot in her forehead. That's what made me think to call you. These look like professional hits."

She turned her attention to the sheet, her mind visualizing the body. A contract killing changed the dynamics of the case. Armed robbers, home invaders sought money, jewelry, electronic devices. The motivations for their actions were easier to determine. Professional killers, however, complicated the investigation. They worked for other people, adding another layer of complexity. No, she was not ready to pursue the possibility of a professional hit. She raised her head toward Reynolds. "I'd like to see the other body."

... ...

After examining the other victim and inspecting the rummaged rooms on the second floor, Cruz, Ashford and Reynolds returned to the kitchen. Hands on her hips and scanning the room, she stood near the table; on the opposite side laid the body. "What have you learned about the victims, detective?"

Detective Reynolds studied his notepad. "Jason and Jane Wilson...age forty and thirty-eight...they both worked at a pharmaceutical company in nearby Reston...research scientists...been married for ten years with one child, a daughter."

Cruz remembered seeing photos of a little girl. One of the bedrooms was decorated in a girl's theme—pink walls, ponies and princesses. She spied a child's handheld video game on the kitchen table. "How old is the daughter?"

"According to what we've been able to dig up so far," he paused to flip a few pages, "she should be around seven years old."

Frowning, Cruz glanced at the detective out of the corner of her eye. "Where is she?"

Reynolds shook his head. "We don't know. She wasn't here if that's what you're getting at. My men have searched every floor and every room of this place. There are signs a small child lives here, but the child wasn't found."

Ashford analyzed his partner. Her face seemed to be aging by the second. "Detective, do you know if the Wilson's have family in the area?"

"As we speak, we're trying to track down the next of kin. We're also checking with the neighbors to see if they know any friends of the Wilson's, in case the girl may be at a friend's house."

Cruz turned away. Placing her interlocked fingers on her head, she gazed at nothing in particular. Her heart was racing. *Was the girl here when her parents were murdered? Did she see it happen? Did the killers see her and take her? Did they—* Cruz could not finish the last thought. *Dear God, let her be okay. Let her be safe and help us find her, Lord.* She spun on her heels and put her hands on her hips. Staring at the table, she envisioned the worst, while listening to Reynolds finish bringing her and Ashford up to speed on the details of the case. She observed the video game. Her eyes never straying from it, she extended her hand toward the men. "I need a rubber glove?"

Reynolds hailed an officer. Moments later, he handed Cruz two rubber gloves. "What is it?"

She donned the gloves and picked up the game. After examining the screen, she pressed one of the console's buttons a few times and shot a look toward the detective. "What was the Wilson's time of death?"

Reynolds licked his finger and swiped it across pages in his notepad. "I have an *estimated* time of death between 6 p.m. and midnight."

"Detective, have any of your men touched this game...played with it or," she swirled her open hand above the device, "done *anything* with it?"

He shook his head. "No, that's not how we do things. My officers are only to secure the scene. The people from the crime lab collect the evidence." He jerked his thumb over his shoulder. "The lab techs arrived right before you. I told them to stay away from the rooms with the bodies, until you had had a chance to see everything for yourself."

Cruz's eyebrows rolled inward. Creases formed on her forehead.

"What's going on, Agent DelaCruz?"

"What time did the first officer arrive on the scene?"

Reynolds checked his notes and replied, "8:58 a.m."

Placing the game on the table, she inspected the room. From a new perspective, her eyes took in every detail of the kitchen—the spoon on the floor, the chair against the counter, the open refrigerator door, a box of cereal on the counter in front of the chair. She tipped her head backward and saw a half-open cupboard door, revealing more cereal boxes. The color drained from her cheeks and her eyes widened. "The girl's in the house—*right now.*" Cruz waved her arms. "Have your men spread out and search the house...go over every square inch of this place...open every door, every closet...search every shelf—"

Reynolds interrupted. "What makes you so sure she's here?"

She pointed at the game. "The last three high scores have today's date. The most recent one has a time stamp of 8:55 a.m., *three minutes* before the first officer showed up."

Ashford pointed at the game. "Those dates and times could be off, Cruz."

"Maybe," she said.

Reynolds shook his head. "I told you, we've gone over every room. There's no little girl."

Cruz rolled her eyes and sighed. "Think back to your childhood, detective. Did you ever play hide and seek? I did. And, I found some *small* places to hide." She held her praying hands in front of her chest. "Please humor me. Have your men—"

"I got it. I got it." Reynolds rushed into the living, issuing commands to his officers.

Cruz motioned. "We'll start in the kitchen." She pointed toward Ashford's half of the room. "Take that side. I'll start here." They moved toward each other, opening and closing every door. Coming to where the counter made a right angle, Cruz pulled on a double-hinged door. Two sections opened to form a wide door. Struggling in her tight-fitting skirt, she went to one knee before bending at the waist and peering inside the darkened cavity. She squinted. Once her eyes adjusted to the dimness, she clutched her chest and gasped.

∞ ∞ ∞ ∞ ∞ ∞ ∞

Go to my author page to continue reading Defense of Innocents.

Made in the USA
Monee, IL
23 March 2021